Protector of My Heart

Justus Roux

ISBN 0-9754080-1-1
Copyright © 2004 Erotictales Publication
All rights reserved

Protector of My Heart

To everyone that has believed in me I can never thank you enough.

Justus Roux

Prologue:

Malka a primitive planet, its inhabitants very similar to those on earth, where two clans of Barbarian warriors fight for supremacy; but it is this fight that threatens to eradicate this race of beings.

A strange disease ravished this land wiping out almost half of the females on the planet. Even more precious female lives were lost in the battles between the Dascon and Larmat clans. Hakan the leader of the Dascon clan turned to the Rundal for help. The Rundal are a highly evolved race of beings who have peacefully shared lands with the Dascon tribes agree to help and set out to find a race of beings similar to the barbarian warriors. Though their search was long the Rundal find a planet with females that may be compatible with the large barbarian warriors. Hakan reluctantly prepares to send his son Niro to this watery planet to acquire two females and bring them back to Malka. Though he fears for his only son's safety, the urgent need for females must take precedence. The fate of the barbarian race depends on if their warriors can mate successfully with these two females.

Justus Roux

Chapter 1

"Niro, it is important that you only take a small group of warriors with you." Hakan said. He looked upon his son with a father's pride. Niro has proven himself in several battles as well as winning the trials two years in a row. Now for the first time Hakan was fearful for his son. The Rundal will be taking Niro and a few other warriors to a totally different planet in their metal beast.

"I understand father." Niro strapped on his knife to his thigh, more out of a force of habit then anything. He knew the Rundal were a peaceful race. "Many of my men have not lain with a female in many months; this could be a dangerous thing for the people of this watery planet."

"Remember only bring back two females. We need to see if they can survive on this planet first before we import more."

"This is wise, father."

"Indeed. I will not have the blood of another female on my conscience."

"Rage clouded your judgment father. That was a long time ago." Niro hated to see his father like this. He knew his father was sorry for not putting an end to the battles that constantly erupted between the two clans. A man who continues to wrestle his own conscience is a truly remorseful man.

"Take Saa and two lesser warriors with you. This should be enough to secure two females." Hakan placed his hand firmly on Niro's shoulder. "Make the females want to come with you, but if necessary force them too."

"I will be as gentle as possible." Niro tied back his long black hair. Men on Malka wore their hair very long, usually running the length of their backs.

"Be careful of their males, we know not the kind of warriors they are."

"I will try not to shed any blood father."

"Yours and theirs, Niro." Hakan gave Niro that stern look, the one that told Niro that his father was deadly serious.

"I will try." Niro bowed his head to Hakan and headed out of the royal chambers.

"Niro." Kelila, his mother ran up to him. Niro fell into her waiting arms. "I was so afraid I had missed you." Kelila cupped his face in her hands. Kelila stood at six feet tall and she had to look up at her large son. His impressive frame was six foot six and he was only average size for a Malka male. She smiled warmly at him; he reminded her so much of his father. Not only because they both were very handsome, but because both had such a strong since of self and duty. She knew Niro would make a good ruler when his time came.

"I would have sought you out mother." He smiled down at her warmly.

"Your father did say to bring only two females back, right?"

"Yes, don't worry mother, I will try to make the journey a pleasant one for the females."

"That is another thing, Niro." She gently led him over to the side of the hall. She didn't want any other warrior hearing them. "Don't take the females against their will." She fussed with his hair feeling a bit awkward speaking of such things with her son. "The females will be frightened and being ravished by a large warrior well…let's say might traumatize them. "

"I will not force myself upon either of them, mother, and I will make sure none of my men will either." Niro knew this would be a hard promise to keep. It had been a long time since he has had the pleasure of a female, the same with his men. But he would try this was the best he could offer his mother.

She lightly kissed him on the cheek and let him go on his way. Being a female on Malka was both a blessing and a curse. No female was ever lonely on this planet, with there being something like twenty men per every woman. But the ones who were not joined with a male, well they were treated like prizes and they had to be constantly on the look out. If she had not a male to protect her any man could ravish her. Kelila looked into the throne room, she was lucky she had a male, but these foreign women would not.

Justus Roux

Chapter 2

Robin sighed looking out the kitchen window as she mindlessly washed the dishes. Life wasn't living up to her dreams. A nowhere job, no children, and a husband who was as romantic as a stick. Charles, her husband was a practical man, wasting money or time on frivolous romantic gestures was beyond him.

Robin closed her eyes, her body stiffened to Charles' touch. "What's wrong did I scare you?" He laughed.

"Yeah." She placed the last dish into the strainer.

"Come on baby, let's go in the bedroom." He rubbed his hard cock against her back. "Got something for you."

Robin knew it was useless to say no. He would pick at her until she said yes anyways. They headed into the bedroom and like always, he took off his clothes and climbed into bed waiting for her. She knew exactly what was going to happen before it did. She tried for years to get him to loosen up, try new things, but not her Charlie. He squeezed her breast a couple of times, rubbed her clit for a few seconds then climbed on top of her.

"Look at me Charlie, say something nasty to me." Robin purred as she grinded her hips into him.

"Hey, you know I don't like talking during sex. Relax baby and enjoy the ride." Charlie went back to his thrusting. A few moments later, he grunted and then rolled off her. "Like that?" He smiled at her.

Robin just smiled back at him. She watched him get out of the bed, pull on his pants, and head out to the living room. The sound of the TV clicking on grated at her. Nothing was getting through to him. The hints, books, magazine articles, hell coming straight out and telling him none of it worked. Robin was starved for romance, starved for some hot sex.

She picked up her book she had been reading the night before. "Take me away, Barbarian man." She laughed looking at the cover. A well-muscled warrior wearing little to nothing was standing in front of a smaller woman. His sword was drawn, ready to defend his love. Robin opened the book to where she left off and began reading.

A few hours later, she closed the book and stretched out on the bed. The floor under her shook violently. "Charlie!!" She cried out as she huddled in the bed.

"Shhh, calm down woman, a little earth quake nothing more." Charlie climbed into bed with her.

"An earthquake in Ohio."

"It has happen, see there it is over." Charlie patted her on the hand and climbed out of bed.

A bright light flooded the bedroom. "What the hell…" Charlie said as he covered his eyes. "You stay here." He went to his gun cabinet and grabbed his rifle. "I mean it, Robin, stay here."

"Yes my warrior man." Robin giggled.

Protector of My Heart

"What....never mind, just stay here." Charlie hurried out of the room and headed for the kitchen door. "Damn hunters and their stupid spot lights. Didn't they know that is illegal?" Charlie cursed and mumbled as he put his jacket on. But before he could reach the door it burst into pieces, sending wood shards everywhere.

Charlie gripped his gun and quickly pointed at the door. He fired two shots, whoever broke his door will be paying a high price, he thought. When he opened his eyes, his jaw dropped. Standing before him were four of the largest men he had ever seen. They had large swords and wore only what appear to be loincloths.

"This isn't fucking Halloween." Charlie raised his gun again but before he could fire, the largest of the men knocked the gun from his hand.

"It is but a weaker male." Saa said grabbing a handful of Charlie's short dark hair. "He doesn't even have his warrior's length."

"My what...." Charlie punched and kicked at the large man but was easily thrown aside as though he weighed as little as a child.

"Mmmm, I smell pussy." Niro growled standing next to the bedroom door.

"Get the fuck away from there!!" Charlie dragged himself up only to be met by a strong fist, it knocked him out instantly.

"Why didn't we just slay him?" Saa said breathing in the air. "I want that pussy."

Niro stopped Saa from breaking the door. "I will gather the female, you wait." Niro's hand tightened on the hilt of his sword when he heard Saa's growls.

Niro waited for Saa to back off then rammed open the door. He just stood there as his eyes feasted on the small woman's body.

Robin backed up toward the end of the room, shaking her head in disbelief. She was face to face with a barbarian is the only word that popped into her mind. He was a solid wall of muscle, stood at least six and a half feet tall, his black hair was thick, and hung down the length of his back. His face was the most handsome thing she had ever seen, chiseled features, full lips and dazzling green eyes. He wore only a leather loin cloth, she had to do a second take on that fact, metal wrist bands and had a large knife strap to his thigh.

"I must be dreaming..." Robin backed up even more as the large man moved toward her.

"I am Niro and I mean you know harm." He said his voice deep and velvety.

"Oh look you can speak English how convenient for me, huh. Oh why ain't I waking up?" Robin moved to the other side of the bed.

"Your language was not hard to learn, it is very similar to mine." He walked to her, his cock already becoming hard looking at the little woman. Never had he seen such a delicate looking female. She came up to the middle of his chest, very soft and curvy, large breasts, his eyes couldn't leave her breasts.

His eyes watched her tits bounce in the flimsy cover she had on. He licked his lips wanting to feast on those tits. He forced his eyes to her face. She was very pretty, soft features, blue sparkling eyes and those lips ummm... he hurried to her causing her to step back. He reached for her and threw her over his shoulder. This one was his.

"Put me down!!" Robin pounded on his back.

Protector of My Heart

"You must come with me."

"What have you done with Charlie?" She stopped fighting what was the point she obviously wasn't hurting the big ox.

"Your male is no longer your concern."

"Niro." A deep male's voice boomed in her ear. The next thing Robin felt was someone burying their face in her pussy. She felt a wet, hungry tongue lap and bathe every inch of her pussy.

"Saa, get back to the ship." Niro pushed him away from Robin.

"Mmm, her pussy is sweet." Saa buried his face back into her pussy. Niro pushed him away again and headed into the kitchen. He had to get the female back onto the ship.

"Charlie!" Robin cried out as fear started to take over her.

"Your male will live, but you are coming with me." Niro said giving her a gentle slap on her ass. He saw the hungry look on Saa's face and knew it was time to leave. Damn it he was going to have to fight Saa for the woman, there was no way around it. He hated fighting his friend but he sure the hell would for this sweet smelling pussy.

Robin felt really hot and saw only white for a few seconds when her eyes adjusted she was inside a metal chamber. What was odd about it was that it looked like a bedroom. She felt the soft furs under her and almost started to laugh. The fur covered bed and weapons hanging around looked terribly out of place in this ……. Robin bolted up. "A freaking spaceship!! There is no way….I mean no fucking way." She jumped out of the bed and headed over to the metal door. She looked everywhere for the switch. "Damn it! There is always some kind of button or something in the movies."

The sound of swords clashing caught her attention. She pressed her ear against the door. The sound of metal and men grunting was all she could hear. Then it stopped. She pressed herself closer against the door straining to hear. The next thing she knew she was on the floor face down.

"What are you doing?" Niro said. He was a bit shocked when she fell out of the door when he opened it. He licked his lips seeing her bare ass exposed to him, nice and round, just liked he preferred.

Robin quickly pulled her robe down over her ass and stood up. All she could see was a wall of muscle before her. The smell of man invaded her nose causing her pussy to dampen. "Where are you taking me?" She walked back into the room.

"Malka." Niro's eyes drank in all of her. His cock so hard, it ached. There was no way he was going to keep his promise. He had just fought Saa for the right to choose which of the two females he wanted to have. He decided on this dark haired beauty.

Robin looked up at Niro she could see the hunger in his eyes. Her eyes drifted down to his leather loincloth. Oh yeah he was thinking what she thought he was thinking. His cock had to be enormous to create such an impressive bulge.

"Stay away from me." Robin climbed on the bed and huddled in the corner. Everything began to sink in. She was in what appeared to be a spaceship and was headed for somewhere called Malka. Her eyes darted up and down Niro's large frame. This impressive wall of muscles could do whatever he wanted to her and she would be powerless to stop it. Fear, confusion and a real doubt of her own sanity engulfed her.

Niro saw the fear in her face. He would be rattled too if someone plucked him off his planet and whisked him away to another. He carefully sat down on the bed and tried to ignore his painful erection. "It will be alright." He said in a quiet voice. "I will not hurt you." He petted her lightly. Her hair, a rich brown color that hung down to her shoulders, felt so soft in his hands. "You will like Malka." He didn't know what to say or what to do to ease her fear.

Robin looked up into his dazzling green eyes; the gentleness in them was soothing in a strange way. "Why me, why take me?"

"You were the first female of child bearing age we came across." Niro was fighting hard not to ravish her. He wanted to bury his cock deep inside her warm, wet pussy.

"Oh lucky me, can't win the lottery but I am chosen for this." She started to cry this can't be real, it just can't.

"No, No, don't do that." Niro gently wiped away the falling tears. He groaned softly when Robin wrapped her arms around him seeking some kind of comfort. He placed his arms around her and just enjoyed the softness and warmth of her body. He could feel her tears dampen his chest. "Don't cry, it pains me to see a female crying."

"I am sorry I shouldn't have done that. I mean I don't even know you." Robin couldn't take her eyes off his full lips.

"I will leave you alone now. You probably need time to think." Niro couldn't control himself much longer. But he wouldn't allow himself to ravish this frighten woman, not now anyways.

"Thank you Niro."

Hearing his name coming from her lips almost caused him to lose the little control he had left. "What is your name?" He asked.

"Robin." She replied quietly.

"Robin." He bowed his head and left quickly before he changed his mind and fucked the hell out of her right now.

Chapter 3

Niro stomped down the corridors of the ship. The demands of his cock were almost overwhelming. He drew his sword when he approached one of the lesser warriors. Instinctively the younger warrior readied himself. Niro had to do something to take his mind off the female.

The two sparred until the younger warrior couldn't give Niro anymore of a challenge. "Good fight." Niro said as he helped the warrior to his feet. He placed his sword back into its sheath and walked away.

As he walked passed the chamber that held the other female he heard moaning and grunting. "Damn it!" He growled opening the door. Saa was fucking the hell out of the little red-haired woman. He had her down on all fours taking her from behind. The look of pleasure on the little woman's face sent a surge of renewed lust through Niro. He cursed again and headed out of the door straight for Robin's room.

Robin sat on the large bed wrapped up in one of the animal furs. She was trying to picture Malka . Was it like earth? Those barbarians seemed human enough. Maybe a bit larger than earth males but still everything else seemed to be normal. What about Charlie? This question bothered her the most. She was sure he would miss her, hell he probably had the police looking for her now. But would she miss him? Robin tightened the fur closer to her when she realized the answer was no, she won't miss him.

"Robin." Niro said quietly as he entered the chamber. He was trying so hard to control his lust, but it was a losing battle. He had to have her.

"Niro, how much longer until we get to Malka?" She followed his movements with her eyes as he crawled onto the bed. The fire that burnt in his eyes ignited her body. She was more afraid of her own body's response to the look in his eyes than anything else.

He went to the middle of the bed and got up on his knees. His eyes never left her as he untied his covering, and threw the leather cloth onto the floor. Robin's eyes were unable to leave his large cock; it was thick and hard and seemed to be beckoning her to feel it.

"What are you doing?" She managed to get out.

"Readying for sport." Niro growled. "Remove your coverings." He said in a stern voice.

"Excuse me." She tightened the furs around her.

"Remove them willingly or I will rip them from your body."

Robin was frightened and turned on by his deep commanding voice. "Don't hurt me." She quietly said letting the fur slip down her shoulder. With shaking hands, she untied her robe.

"I won't hurt you, female." Niro took deep breaths to calm himself or otherwise he might hurt the small woman. The timid way she removed the robe then her hands trying to cover her beautiful body, almost as if she was ashamed of her body, puzzled him.

"Why do you try to hide such a wondrous body?" Niro moved closer to her and gently removed her hands from her breasts.

"Wondrous, I don't think so." Robin tried placing her hands back up to her breasts but Niro again gently moved them out of the way. Robin felt so awkward kneeling there naked before him. She was never comfortable in her own skin.

"Mmmm." Niro purred lifting her up so he could suck on her erect nipple.

"Hey…wait…" Robin couldn't help but latch onto his head and pull him closer as he suckled. His hair was so soft in her hands; his mouth felt so good feeding on her breast. His hands cupped her ass and pulled her closer to his hard body. The hardness of him felt incredible against her. His hunger for her made her feel sexy and beautiful. She arched her head back leaning more into his hungry mouth, when the moan escaped her lips it caused him to suck harder and more frantic on her breast.

He lifted her up, urging her to wrap her legs around his shoulders so he could taste her sweet pussy. "Niro." She gasped as he buried his tongue into her pussy. He licked and sucked on her clit wanting to taste the sweetness of her. His strong arms steadied her so she wouldn't fall over.

"Niro, oh yes…yes…" She began to grind onto his face causing them to fall over onto the bed. He wallowed his face in her pussy wanting it to be covered with her juice as his tongue continued to bathe her pussy. Robin tightened her hands in his hair and pushed him closer to her. He responded by burying his tongue deep into her pussy, darting in and out, fucking it with his tongue. "Oh, yes… don't stop, please don't stop." Robin said breathy as her orgasm build. "Please don't stop!" She arched her back as her orgasm exploded. She moved side to side on the bed wanting his tongue to go deeper in her. And as if he knew what she wanted, he buried his tongue deep in her, circling it around and around, feeling it pulse against his tongue. He growled and eagerly drank down her juice as it flowed into his mouth.

Robin laid there with her legs wide open as he tenderly lapped at her clit and pussy lips. "Let me taste you." Robin quietly said. She looked down into his face, her own juice glistening from it. Their eyes locked as his tongue rolled over her clit. "Please Niro let me taste you." Robin had never tasted a man's cock. Charlie believed oral sex was nasty and had no place in their bedroom. But now looking down at Niro as he tenderly licked on her pussy, Robin couldn't see anything nasty at all about it.

Niro groaned and stood up. He could have eaten her pussy all night. He watched as she timidly reached out for his cock. The delicious look on her face as she gently stroked him, trying to get her hand to go around his thick cock made precum squirt out. His balls twitched when she gingerly licked at the head of his cock cleaning off the precum. Her tongue was warm and wet and felt wonderful as she licked up and down his shaft. "Take me into your mouth." Niro said as he gently guided her mouth back to the head of his cock. He watched as his cock began to disappear into her mouth. The warm, wet, sucking, and licking of her mouth felt incredible to him. He leaned his head back and focused on the sensation of it. He began to thrust into her mouth slowly, not sure how much of his cock she could swallow. He looked down and watched as she tried to take more and more of his cock into her mouth. "Say something...." He whispered. Her muffled moan caused him to thrust harder into her mouth causing her to gag. He released her head and allowed her to set the pace. He leaned his head back and closed his eyes trying to hold

Protector of My Heart

back from cumming. This was heavenly and he never wanted it to stop. Her eagerness combine with her unsureness was incredible. He quickly looked down when he heard the popping sound of his cock leaving her hungry mouth. He groaned feeling her wet tongue bathing his balls as her hand stroked at his cock. "Take them into your mouth, suck oh please suck." Niro pushed her face closer to his balls. "Yes, mmm, yes." He growled as she took as much of his balls as she could into her mouth and gently sucked on them. Never had he felt such a sensation. "Feed on my cock some more, female." He pulled her up again to the head of his cock and she eagerly began sucking on him. "I want to feed you….now…" He bobbed her head up and down on his cock making sure he wouldn't let her take more than she wanted. He felt his cock sliding down her throat as she took more and more of it into her mouth. He quickly looked down feeling his balls tighten. He wouldn't cum yet, oh no, not yet he wanted to see if she could take all of him down her throat. "More, yes, more." He pushed down on her head wanting all of his cock down her throat. When he felt her nose against his pubic hair, he couldn't hold his orgasm back. He bobbed her head faster on his cock as his orgasm build. "Yes, Yes, ahh female, you glorious female, Yess!!!!" He screamed as his orgasm exploded violently filling her mouth full of his juice. He looked down at her and gently caressed her cheek. "Thank you." He whispered stroking her cheek before he fell onto the bed next to her. It had been so long since he had an orgasm that good.

    He reached up and pulled her down to him. Oh, he wasn't done yet. He needed to feel her pussy. He rolled over and gently laid on top of her.

"Wait." Robin looked deep into his eyes. "Kiss me first."

Niro's heart literally skipped a beat hearing such an innocent request. He rolled off her stunned for a moment. "A kiss." He said.

"Yes." Robin was confused by the nervous look in his eye. This man had just fucked her mouth and now he was getting shy.

"I don't ….I …never just kissed…a female before." Niro had only just taken females before fuck them hard and fast. Use their bodies as long as they would permit, none had ever requested a kiss.

Robin gently took his face into her hands then slowly brushed her lips against his. "Our lips will taste one another, and then allow your tongue to explore my mouth." Robin didn't quite know how to explain a kiss. Niro followed her lead, letting his lips find hers, his tongue dance with hers and soon he was lost in their deep kiss. His cock grew very hard the longer they held that kiss. He rolled her over and gently entered her, he arched up, and growled feeling her velvety and tight pussy totally consumed his cock. Slowly he filled her wanting her to get use to him. Her pussy was so tight compared to the Malka females would she be able to take all of him inside. He looked down to make sure he wasn't causing her any pain.

Robin wrapped her legs around his waist, never had she felt so full. His cock was stretching her almost to the point of pain. She looked up into his face seeing him trying to remain under control. He didn't want to hurt her, she soon realized. This sweet gesture warmed her. This man barely knew her and yet he treated her with more gentleness than Charlie ever did.

Protector of My Heart

"Are you ready?" Niro asked. Robin nodded her head. Niro drove every last inch of his cock into her filling her completely full. Slowly he thrust, holding his weight with his arms; he didn't want to crush her. He looked down into her face the pleasure he saw there heightened his want. He thrust harder and faster, she matched his intensity. "Take your pleasure female, for I am about to take mine."

Robin knew what he meant; she was already on her way to bliss. Niro felt her pussy clamp down on his cock then tightened and release. He drove his cock deeper and faster as his own orgasm hit him. He continued to thrust until all his juice had come out. He collapsed down onto her not wanting to leave the warmth of her.

"You are crushing me." Robin said trying to push him off.

"Forgive me." He rolled over and pulled her to him. "Sleep now." He pulled the furs over the top of them and smiled when she snuggled down against his chest.

Chapter 4

"She is so small."

Robin's eyes popped open upon hearing a woman's voice. There standing next to Niro was a most beautiful woman. She had to be six feet tall, her body was strong but still very feminine, and her hair was tied back in one long braid that reached her waist. However, it was the eyes, the same dazzling green eyes that Niro has that caught Robin's attention.

"Robin, this is my mother Kelila she will help you dress." Niro gently kissed his mother's cheek then left the room.

"I have brought your coverings." Kelila's smiled warmly. "I am afraid we will have to alter them a bit. Are all females from your planet so small?"

"Some are your height." Robin climbed out of bed wrapping an animal fur around her. Kelila's clothing was striking. The long gown was made of a shimmering fabric that seemed to change color from light blue to white as Kelila moved. Her shoulders were bare but the rest of her was covered except for the slit in the front of the dress, which showed glimpses of her leg as she walked. Her shoes looked very similar to sandals but were made of what look like a soft fabric.

Robin ran her hand over the fabric of her covering, it felt like silk but softer and lighter. She was amazed that she couldn't see through such a light fabric.

"It is made from the Balma Tree's leaves. I will show you this tree later if you wish." Kalila said as she cut about six inches from the length of the covering.

"I have to admit I am a bit relieved that you are not wearing what Niro is." Robin let the fur fall to the floor as Kalila wrapped the covering around her. The fabric felt wonderful against her skin.

"It would not be wise for a woman to run around half-naked." Kalila smiled as she looked over Robin.

"Why is that?" Robin allowed Kalila to brush her hair. She felt completely safe around this woman.

"Our warriors would be distracted." Kalila turned Robin around. "You have much to learn, please listen to what Niro and I tell you." Kalila handed Robin a looking glass. "You are very lucky; Niro wants to be your protector."

"My protector?" Robin liked the little jewels Kalila placed in her braided hair.

"He will protect you from the other warriors."

"Why would I need protection?"

"Come sit." Kalila sat down on the bed, Robin sat next to her.

"On Malka there are too few females, on top of this Malka males are a very amorous bunch to begin with." Kalila turned to Robin and gently took her hand. "I don't know what life for a female was like on your planet, but here females are treated like prizes."

"Prizes?"

"We are given away as prizes to deserving warriors. Males may mate with any female that hasn't been joined.

Protector of My Heart

So females without a protector have to fight off the warriors themselves. You have seen my son. Malka males are very large, so a female has little chance of defending herself."

"Oh God." Robin stood up. She didn't want to be treated like a prize and she sure the hell didn't want to be a damn blow up doll for these flipping warriors.

"Don't worry, Niro will protect you. He is the best warrior in all of Dascon." Kalila pulled Robin back down to a seated position. "When you have joined, being a female on this planet is a wonderful thing. You are treated like a precious jewel, and no warrior would dare touch the mate of another."

"Why?"

"They would face death. When a warrior challenges a protector the two fight but no one dies. When a warrior dare challenges or even touches the mate of another, they fight until the death. Most warriors respect the joining and don't bother the woman in the first place."

"This is confusing."

"You will learn. Now let's go meet Niro and your fellow female."

ଓଓଓ

Robin headed off the ship and down to a corridor of a large building. Niro and three other men waited at the end of the corridor. Standing beside the largest of the men was a red-haired woman about Robin's height.

"Oh thank God." The woman screeched as she ran over to Robin. "Please tell me you are from earth too." The woman had a strong grip on Robin's arms.

"Yes I am. My name is Robin Stevens." She was so relieved looking at the red haired woman. She didn't feel so alone now.

"I am Sabrina Taylor." She hugged Robin tight. "What the hell is going on? Saa hasn't told me too much only that he is my protector."

"I don't know to much more than that."

"Don't worry you will learn." Kelila gently pulled the women apart. "My best advice would be to listen to your protectors." Both women nodded and followed her to the men.

Robin looked up at Saa; he had to be a good two inches taller than Niro. He was dressed the same but the metal bracelets he wore had different symbols than Niro's on them. His hair was long, dark, and tied back with a leather strap. His face was harder looking than Niro's but still he was rather handsome in his own right. The thing that caught Robin's eye was the long scar that ran down his left arm.

"A blade in battle." Saa commented when he noticed Robin looking at his scar.

"Excuse me?" Robin looked up at him

"This is from an enemy's blade."

"Did you do worse to him?"

"I took his head." Saa gripped his sword hilt when he heard Niro growling at him. "Calm yourself Niro; your female was curious about my scar."

Robin saw Saa relax as Niro quieted down. Niro placed himself between Saa and Robin. "You are to close to him, little one." Niro said as he pulled her closer to him.

"Bring the females back to the leader's hut, they have much to learn." Kelila said. She watched both men scare off the two lesser males. A warrior's growl was not to be taken lightly for this was the only warning he gave to another male.

Robin's eyes darted everywhere. The corridor opened up into a large open space. Many people, mostly males wandered about going into different corridors. "This is like an airport." Robin whispered to Sabrina.

She stayed close to Niro as they headed down another corridor. At the end were two males dressed like Niro holding spears. "Niro." Both men bowed their heads.

Robin looked up at Niro and watched as he nodded his head toward them and continued forward. "Oh…" Robin exclaimed looking at the large horse like creature that was harness to the carriage. "That is the biggest, strangest looking horse I have ever seen." The beast had two tails, soft looking fur, and pointy teeth and was as big as three earth horses put together. "A horse from hell." She added.

"Horse?" Niro asked.

"That thing." Robin pointed at the creature. It roared almost like a lion causing Robin to jump back behind Niro.

"This is a Bamk. It will take us where we need to go."

"A Bamk, well that name fits it. Don't you have cars, trains ah, airplanes?"

"We have no such things here." Niro helped her up into the wooden carriage. The carriage was finely crafted with all sorts of jewels covering the outside of it and the same symbol on the door that was on Niro's bracelet.

"But…we were just in a spaceship." Robin was completely confused. How could a race that built the spaceship have no modern means of transportation?

"The ship was made by the Rundal. You will meet them later."

"What does that mean?" Robin pointed at the symbol on Niro's bracelet.

"This is the symbol of the Dascon clan." Niro pointed at the symbol that looked like a dragon. "And this is a symbol of my lineage." He pointed at the symbol that looked like two crossed flaming swords with a gold band circling them.

"Is your father an important man?" Robin looked at the other men who had begun to laugh loudly.

"His father is the leader of the Dascon clan, female." Saa chuckled.

"Then you are…"

"Your protector." Niro smiled warmly at her. He pulled her closer to him so he could feel the heat of her body. "Look at your new home, little one." He pointed to the window.

"Wow…" Was all she could say looking out at the beautiful landside. Trees with leaves that look like silk, in various colors covered the hillsides.

"The Balma Tree." Kelila added.

The hillsides gave way and unveiled a large city nestled in a valley. An enormous mountain range could just be seen in the distance. In the center of this town stood a large structure, the towers shimmered and gave warmth to the whole building.

"The town of Dascon." Niro said as they entered the gateway.

"It is the main village for the people of the Dascon lands." Kelila added.

Robin looked everywhere trying to soak it all in. All the men were dressed like Niro and what few women she did see were as big as Kelila and dressed like her. Robin smiled at the group of children who were waving at the carriage.

"Our children are our greatest treasure." Kelila said as she waved at the children.

The closer they came to the two large towers Robin noticed they seemed to be covered with diamonds or something very similar. "They are beautiful." Robin commented.

"They are a gift from my father to my mother, so she would always see light and beauty when she looked out her window in the morning." Niro said.

"Very generous gift from your father." Kelila smiled.

"Yeah, I would say so." Robin added. The only gift Charlie ever got her was kitchen appliances or other stuff she could use around the house. Gifts should be useful, he would always tell her as he handed them to her.

Robin saw the large wooden doors opening and a group of men carrying spears headed for the carriage.

"Niro, your father awaits you." One said.

"Niro, may I ask you a question." Robin said as he helped her down from the carriage.

"Feel free to ask me anything, little one."

"Isn't your mother like the queen, you know since your father is the leader and all? Why do all these guys act like she isn't here?"

"A male wouldn't dare speak to my mother."

"Why?"

"My father would kill him."

"So your mother can't talk to any other males." Robin felt Niro's arm go around her and his hand gently pressing into the small of her back as he led her inside.

"A male may talk with my mother if she talks to him first."

"But if he talks with her first, your father would have him executed."

"My father would cut off the male's head himself, if a male spoke with my mother if she didn't want his attention."

"That is a little harsh, isn't it?"

"Not harsh, little one, necessary. You will learn this in time. Now come you must meet my father." Niro gently pressed his hand into her lower back and urged her forward.

ର୍ଷର୍ଷର୍ଷ

Robin couldn't believe the beauty of the leader hut. "This isn't like any hut I ever saw. This is more like a palace." Robin whispered to herself. The wood walls were finely detailed and the veneer of the wood range from a rich brown to a blonde color. The stones that made up the floor sparkled as though they had diamond dust in them. Some of the floors were black and others grey. The furniture was made of wood and had various furs as coverings; they looked warm and comfortable.

Robin grew nervous when they reached a room that had two large stone pillars by it, as if to mark this room's importance. Robin watched Kelila run into the room and throw herself into the arms of a very large man who bared a striking resemblance to Niro.

"They are so small." Hakan noted looking over the two women. "Is mating possible with them?" He looked over at Niro.

"Yes, if done carefully."

"You know this for a fact."

"Yes father."

Robin couldn't help but blush. She felt Hakan's fingers under her chin as he lifted her eyes to meet his. "What is your name?" His smile was as warm as Niro's.

"Robin Stevens, your highness… kingly person… leader dude."

"Just call me Hakan this will be fine." He ran his hand down her braid. "Your hair will have to be grown out." He went over to Sabrina and looked her over.

"Are you females feeling okay, does are climate agree with you?"

"A little warmer than I am use to." Robin replied.

"It is always warm here. But this I am sure you will get use to."

Well that explained why all the men ran around half-naked and the fabric of her covering was so light, Robin thought.

"Go get them settled and let them rest. The Rundal will be joining us at the feast later on." Hakan watched them all leave. "They are very small." Hakan walked up to his large chair and sat down. "Our males may hurt them during sport."

"Don't worry, if the red-haired one survived sport with Saa I would say these earth females are a lot sturdier than they look." Kalila sat down on his lap.

"True, Saa has been known to make a female spend days recovering and that Sabrina walked in here on her own." Hakan grabbed Kalila roughly by the arms as he stood up. He bent her over the chair arm and pulled off her covering. He quickly undid his leather covering and rammed his cock into her pussy. He held her arms behind her back with one hand and grabbed her braid with the other causing her to arch her back. Kalila loved it when he took her so roughly. She felt his cock slam into her over and over, heard him grunting and growling as he rode her faster and faster. "Take your pleasure woman." He growled. Kalila grinded her hips back into him as her orgasm hit. "Oh yeah cum my female." He rode her harder as his own orgasm exploded. His roar echoed through the room. He collapsed down on her. "Oh I have missed you."

"I was only gone a day, you didn't have time to miss me." She giggled trying to push him off.

"Even one day without my cock buried deep inside you is to long." He reluctantly pulled his cock out and put back on his covering. "Niro wants to be protector for that little dark-haired one?"

"Yes and I couldn't be happier. Finally he has chosen a mate." Kelila secured her covering.

"Remember woman she has to accept him first. We know no male can best him at a fight, so he will prove the strongest male to her. But I wonder if this matters to this imported female. "

"Niro said her male on earth was pathetically weak so I don't think it does matter to them."

"How then does a female choose her mate on that planet?"

"I don't know, I shall have to ask them." Kelila leaned into his warm embrace. "Niro will prove himself to her. Let's not worry about this now, she has just arrived, and besides we must prepare for the Rundal's visit."

Chapter 5

Niro escorted Robin into a large chamber. "This is my chamber." He said gripping her braid in his hand. His cock was already hungry for her. He was supposed to take her to the dressing chamber but his cock had other ideas.

"Nice, very nice." Robin said looking around. The large bed they were standing next to caught her eye first. It was made of wood, had something that resembled a mattress but fluffier and furs were thrown over it. She also felt Niro's hand pulling on her braid.

"I want the pleasure of your mouth again, little one." Niro lowered her down to her knees by pulling on the braid.

"That is nice but..." She watched as he unfastened his covering and let it fall to the floor. "Hey wait."

"Pleasure me, little one." He firmly gripped his large cock in one hand and pulled her head closer with the other. "Open your mouth." He grunted. His cock ached just feeling her breath upon it.

Robin felt the head of his cock pressing on her lips. The urgent need in his voice coupled with his forceful actions was really turning her on. She allowed him to push his cock into her mouth. She suckled gently at first wanting to make him wait. Both of his hands were now tangled in her hair as he thrust his cock deeper into her mouth.

"Yes female, suckle me, just like that, oh yes." Niro pushed down on her head needing her to take more of his cock into her mouth. The sucking noises she made were driving him mad. He sat down on the edge of the bed still holding her head firmly to him. He watched as she intensified her efforts; her tongue lapped at the head of his cock before she would swallow all of him again. "This is heavenly." He cried as he fell back into the bed, his hands gently holding her head wanting to feel it bob on his cock. He brought both of his feet up on the bed when she lowered down to his balls. He wanted her to have full access to him to do whatever she wanted. He would do anything she wanted at this moment. If she told him to kill someone, he would grant her request as long as her tongue, lips and mouth kept doing what they were doing to him. He felt her tongue bathe his balls with long, wet strokes. His hand went to his cock and began to stroke when she licked at the area right under his balls.

"Tell me to stop if I do something that makes you feel uncomfortable." Robin said she smiled when Niro grunted and pushed her face back down to his balls.

Niro felt Robin cup his ass as she continued to lick his balls and inner thighs. Her tongue journeyed lower running up the line of his ass. Niro gasped and raised up to watch her, he could only see the top of her head as her tongue explored areas no woman has ever tasted on him before. He fell back onto the bed as her tongue circled around his rosebud. Her hand stroked his cock at the same time and at the same speed, her tongue circled.

"I am going to take my pleasure female...oh yes!!" He roared his cum shooting into the air. "Little one." He said breathing hard as he watched her lick the juice that ran down his cock. "Come here, female." He lifted her up to him with little effort. "Cover my face with your pussy." He positioned her over his face and sat her down firmly on him.

Robin rubbed her pussy on his face as his greedy tongue lapped at her. His nose rubbed against her clit as he grinded her hips into his face. Robin grabbed handfuls of his hair as she rode his face. His tongue darted in and out of her pussy, his nose continued to rub her clit. Her orgasm was intense as she held him firmly to her. "No more Niro." She said climbing off his face.

"I am not done yet." He growled flipping her over then raising her hips up to him. He pushed her head down into the mattress as he rammed his cock into her.

Robin tried to move, needing to push her hips back into him. His cock filled, stretched, and enraptured her. "Niro let me up." She wanted to, no hell needed to grind against him.

"No." He growled pushing her upper body harder into the mattress forcing her ass up higher. "This pussy is mine." He howled riding her harder. "All mine." His hand gripped her hips. "I will kill any warrior that even smells this pussy." He howled louder as he stood up on the bed taking her with him. He held her up with his strong arms, slamming her hips into him. "Take your pleasure female, cum for me." He growled biting her shoulder.

Robin felt his fingers rubbing her clit, him biting her shoulder, the strength of him as he held her up like that. His cock drove into her over and over, harder and faster. "Cum for me female!" He ordered biting her shoulder harder, growling like some wild animal. Robin's orgasm engulfed her causing her to scream his name. She heard herself begging him to cum and fill her full of his juice.

His roar rattled the walls sending a shiver through her as she felt his juice run out of her pussy and down her thighs.

Niro fell into the bed making sure she was on top when they landed. He pulled her close to him and buried his face in her hair. "Did I hurt you, little one?" He sounded remorseful. He lost control. He kissed the bite mark on her shoulder.

"Not to bad." She leaned into his embrace.

"I am so sorry." He hugged her tighter.

"It is alright, Niro. Hum, I rather enjoyed it." She chuckled.

"Tell me if I start to hurt you during sport."

"Sport? That is what, ah that was."

"Yes, now promise me."

"I promise." She snuggled closer loving the heat of his body.

ଔଔଔ

Robin sat in the chair and let the young woman braid up her hair. Sabrina walked in and collapsed onto the chair next to her.

"Saa is going to fuck me to death." Sabrina chuckled.

"Eager is he?"

"That is an understatement." Sabrina leaned in a bit. "His cock is like a freaking cannon. I mean I can't even get my hand around the big ass thing."

Robin couldn't help but laugh. "Tell me is Niro that gifted as well?" Sabrina asked.

"Yes he is."

"All Malka males are very well endowed." The woman doing there hair added.

"What is your name?" Robin asked.

"Dalmace, mate to Neman."

"I'm Robin and this is Sabrina." Robin looked over the woman. She was very tall and well muscled but still very feminine looking. Her rich brown hair was braided up and hung down to her waist. "So you have joined with Neman."

"Yes over a year ago." She smiled. This explains why Niro and Saa acted as though this woman wasn't even in the room. "You are lucky, Robin, Niro will be the next leader of the Dascon clan and is the best warrior. He won the Trials twice. This is a most amazing feat."

"Well, looks like your protector is like the most eligible bachelor here." Sabrina whispered to Robin.

"Of course Saa is a very strong warrior too." Sabrina noticed a blush cross Dalmace's face. "Very skilled in sport as well."

"Oh my protector is a stud muffin." Sabrina laughed.

"Hurry little one, we will be late." Niro said as he entered the room. "You are most beautiful." He smiled warmly.

"You look really good yourself." Robin's eyes lingered on his glorious body. He was wearing some sort of leather vest. The rest of his coverings were the same minus the knife strapped to his thigh. His sword was strapped to his back. Robin suspected that sword was never to far away from him. "Why the vest?"

"Vest?"

"This." Robin ran her hands down the soft leather.

"It was a gift from the Rundal Sasha, so I wear to honor her."

"Oh that's sweet of you." Robin started to feel nervous, how was she supposed to act. Moreover, what the heck did a Rundal look like?

"Niro we must go." Saa said as he kneaded Sabrina's breasts.

"This is no time for sport Saa." Niro gently took Robin by the hand and led her out of the room. He heard the thump against the wall and knew he would have to make an excuse up for his overly horny friend. Though he couldn't blame Saa, he would much rather have his cock buried deep in Robin's sweet pussy then go to the banquet. However, being the next leader his presence was required. Beside the Rundal leader was eager to see the imported female.

Robin heard the beautiful music as they proceeded down the corridor to a large pair of wooden doors. The music was haunting almost heavenly in its tone and unlike anything she heard before. "Where does the music come from?"

Niro pointed up to three old women. One had a strange looking flute like instrument, another had something that looked like a small harp, and the other was singing. Robin couldn't understand the words. "What is she singing?"

"She is singing in Rundal tongue." Niro stopped walking and let Robin look at the music makers. "She is telling the story of one Rundal warrior watching his world blow up as he hovered in a spaceship just beyond. Now with his home gone he must journey with the remaining Rundal and try to find another home. It is important they survive or the Rundal will be no more. There is no time for pain, regret, or grief these will come later. "The singer's voice lightens becoming more joyous, hopeful. Niro watches Robin looking at the singer mesmerized by her voice. "They find a world not very different than their own." Niro feels Robin tighten her grip on his hand. "This world has a strange race of beings, but these beings are not frightened by the Rundal. The Leader learns the language of the Barbarian and communicates. The Barbarians allow the Rundal to live in the mountains, giving to them freely the land, and what they need to survive. The warrior watches as the Barbarian tribes protects the Rundal from invading armies. Golden haired devils the invaders are forever known. The warrior trains with the dark-haired barbarians. They live together in peace." The singer's voice changes back to a hauntingly sad tone. "The warrior looks to the sky and sees his mate and their young dancing in the dust of his home planet. Now it is time to grieve. Now it is time for sadness. Now it is time for regret. Now it is time to remember."

"Did this really happen?" Robin choked back her tears.

"Yes, this is how the Rundal came to our planet. Sasha the mate of the Rundal leader Tomar loves this song." Niro cupped her face. "It is not meant to be a sad song, little one, but a song of remembrance." He gently brushed his lips over her eyes then softly kissed her. "Now come you must meet Tomar and Sasha."

"How can she sing so beautiful?" Robin looked one last time up at the three old women.

"When Malka women age they obtain many talents. Now come." Niro led them up to the large doors that were opened wide inviting all inside the grand hall. The room was enormous; many barbarian warriors roamed around, some with mates others without. The mood was very joyous.

"What are you celebrating?" Robin asked soaking up the atmosphere over the room.

"This is the day the Rundal came to our home." Niro smiled down at her. He was taking much pleasure watching her look around with a child's excitement.

"Niro, there you are. You look beautiful Robin." Kelila greeted them warmly.

"So do you." Robin replied.

"Niro, Tomar wants to meet Robin. He is most eager to see her." Kelila led them through the crowd.

Robin stopped abruptly causing Niro to pull her forward before he realized she had stopped. "What is wrong?" He saw the horrified look in her eyes.

Robin couldn't move. Standing by Hakan was a very large monster. It had the form of a man, but it looked like a large lizard. Its tail had to be at least four feet long, its skin looked rubbery and had a blackish-greenish color to it. However, it was its face; it reminded Robin of a snake. What was worse it looked like it was talking with Hakan.

"What is wrong Robin?" Niro took her into his arms.

"What the hell is that?" She pointed over towards the monster.

"That is Tomar, the Rundal leader."

Robin turned her head when she heard a hissing sound. "Niro, it is so nice to see you again." Robin's eyes open wide seeing the female version of the monster approach Niro. She was speaking but her mouth wasn't moving.

"Sasha." Niro bowed his head toward her. "This is Robin." Robin clung tighter to Niro.

"Don't be afraid." Sasha seemed to be speaking to Robin's mind. The voice was soft almost soothing.

"Forgive her Sasha." Niro held Robin closer feeling her tremble.

"I was unnerved the first time I saw a Barbarian, Niro. I understand how she feels. No offence but I thought your kind were the ugliest things I have ever seen."

Niro chuckled and felt Robin relax in his embrace. "My mate Tomar is most eager to meet you Robin are you alright to join me." Sasha's tail thumped at the floor. Robin noticed Tomar looking toward her now.

"I will be with you little one." Niro whispered as he nuzzled the top of her head.

"I would love to meet the leader of the Rundal." Robin said as she released Niro and headed toward Sasha. Niro smiled, his female was a brave little one.

Robin put her bravest face on, though she was trembling inside. She did not expect the Rundal to look like something straight out of a Sci-fi show. How could these lizard looking beings make something like that spaceship? The closer she got to Tomar the larger he appeared to her. He towered over Sasha and was twice as broad as she was. His body was even more powerful looking than Niro's, which made Robin wonder just who would win a fight between the two.

"Greetings Robin on behalf of all the Rundal." Tomar's voice didn't fit his body. It was soft and pleasant sounding.

"Greetings." Robin bowed her head.

"She looks so similar to your kind." Tomar noted to Hakan. "A bit smaller. I would like to examine her to see if she is indeed compatible to your kind."

"Would this be alright with you Robin?" Kelila asked. She knew Hakan would just hand the poor female over.

"I guess so. It won't hurt will it?"

"It will not hurt at all." Tomar replied.

Robin tried to look up into his face, but it was just too scary to look at.

"Bring her to our lands, Niro. Let her get adjusted first. But bring her before she decides to join."

"Yes, Tomar."

"Now everyone feast it is time to celebrate. Tonight we honor the Rundal, are close allies and friends." Hakan exclaimed.

Niro pulled Robin off to the side. "The Rundal are a very peaceful race." He gently stroked her cheek. "You need not fear them. I know they are difficult to look at, but you heard Sasha we are no eye candy to them either."

"I wish you would have warned me that the Rundal are walking lizard people then I would have been prepared."

"I am sorry little one, to me they don't look scary, but I know them. Your right I should have warned you."

"OH MY GOD!!! What the hell is that thing!!" Both of them turned to the door upon hearing Sabrina scream.

"I am just guessing here but, I think Saa didn't warn Sabrina either." Robin started to laugh. Niro laughed heartily and pulled her into his arms.

Chapter 6

Robin woke up laying in Niro's arms. Sunlight flooded the room dimming the crystals that hung from the walls. Curious Robin quietly crawled out of bed being careful not to wake Niro. She walked over to one of the large crystals. She had been so preoccupied by Niro's lovemaking and all the newness of the world she never noticed that there was no electricity. She did remember the soft glow that filled the room as she and Niro made love last night. Her hand timidly reached out and touched the crystal; it was cool to the touch.

"I wonder if these are all over." Robin quickly put on her covering and headed out of the chamber. Her eyes darted down the hall. Those strange crystals were everywhere. When she reached the end of the hall, she took the door to the left. It led to the outside. The air was warm and fresh smelling so she wandered down the stone path straight to a Balma tree. She reached up and felt one of the large leaves. It was as soft as her covering was; this particular leaf was the same light blue shade as her covering. Her eyes darted up to the two diamond covered towers. The morning light danced off them flooding the surrounding areas with a warm glow.

"Where is your protector?" A deep voice grumbled.

Robin quickly turned around and looked up at the large dark-haired man. "He will be here any minute." She said quickly. She didn't like the look of lust in this barbarian's eyes.

"You lie." He lunged out at her and grabbed her arm pulling her violently to him. "You smell good, female." His hands groped at her as he backed her up to the wall. She felt him tearing at her covering. She kicked and punched at him but it didn't even slow him down. She tried to cry out but he quickly covered her mouth. She felt herself being pushed to the ground and the heavy weight of him on her.

She heard Niro's familiar growl and then felt the large man being pulled violently off her. The sound of a sword being pulled from its sheath caused Robin to hurry up to her feet. She pulled what was left of her covering around her, trying to cover herself. Her whole body shook. She saw the rage in Niro's eyes when she looked over at him.

"You dare touch my female!" Niro bellowed. He tightened his grip on his sword.

"We will see if she stays your female Niro." The man moved closer to him.

"Stay put, little one." Niro instructed keeping his eyes on the other warrior the whole time.

Robin backed up against the wall and watched as their swords clashed. Niro was very fast and dodged the other barbarian's blows easily. This only made the man madder, making him swing his sword erratic. Robin's breath caught when Niro's blade sliced through the belly of the other barbarian, causing him to fall to the ground. "I am the better warrior, now yield." Niro pointed his sword at the other man's throat.

Protector of My Heart

"I yield, you are the better warrior." The man's voice shook.

Niro used the other man's hair to wipe the blood from his blade then he placed it back in its sheath. He hurried over to Robin and scooped her up into his arms.

"Shouldn't you like, call a doctor or something for him?" Robin said seeing the other man laying there on the ground with blood pooling in his hand. Niro hurried inside.

"He will find his own way or he will die. Are you alright little one?" He kicked his chamber door open. Robin could feel his anger.

"I am okay, just a little shaken up." She yelped when he threw her onto the bed.

"You go nowhere without me, do you understand?" Niro circled the bed his eyes never leaving her. His heart stopped when he woke this morning and she was gone. When he saw the other male on top of her…a renewed anger surged through his body.

"I just wanted to look around."

"Do you understand?" His voice boomed through the room.

"Yes." She sat up and moved to the end of the bed.

"Now I must teach you." Niro removed his covering and climbed on the bed. He grabbed her violently and tore her covering off. He pulled her to him so she could look into his face. "Another warrior will have to kill me before I give you to them." His angry growls were filling Robin with an unexpected hunger.

He flipped her over, pushed her head down to the mattress, and lifted her ass up in the air. With one quick thrust, he entered her. His thrusts were hard and violent as his cock pounded at her pussy. "You will never go anywhere with out me again." He growled slapping her ass hard. Robin gasped her ass burn from where his hand struck her. "Tell me you won't." He slapped her ass again. "Tell me female!!"

"I won't go anywhere without you." Robin felt him pull her hands behind her back.

"I am your male. Say it!" He pulled back on her arms.

"You are my male." Robin tried pushing her hips back wanting him to fuck her harder. His growls were filling her body with sensations. "Show me you are the male." She hissed at him trying to ignite his anger more. "Show me Niro."

He leaned his body over, thrusting his cock as hard as he could into her body. "I will tear this fucking pussy apart, female." He roared as he thrust faster. He pulled her hair causing her back to arch. "Take all my cock in you." He could hear their flesh smacking together, feel her lurch forward from the power of his thrusts. "Tell me I am your male." He bit down hard on her shoulder, grunting and growling loudly.

"You are my male, Niro." Robin felt her orgasm burst through her body. She heard herself screaming his name as his cock continued to pound at her pussy.

"No other male will have you. Oh yes, my female!!!" He yelled as his orgasm hit him. He thrust a few more times then released her and pushed her down onto the bed. He stood up and looked down at her. Robin slowly rolled over and looked up at him. He was breathing hard and he just stared at her. "If you disobey me, I will do far worse." He grabbed his covering and put it on then left the room. Robin heard the door lock. She smiled and laid back into the bed.

Protector of My Heart

Robin followed Niro and Kelila around the grounds of the leader hut. Kelila pointed out the various plant life as they passed. By afternoon the sky had turned a brilliant violet. "Oh, that is so beautiful." Robin exclaimed.

"This is caused when the suns start to lower in the sky." Kelila explained.

"Suns?" Robin looked to the west and east and sure enough there were two small suns in the sky. She looked over quickly at Niro when he growled at a passing warrior.

"Have you been challenged yet, my son?" Kelila asked.

"By one." Niro grabbed Robin's hand and pulled her closer to him. "She decided to go for a walk without me and drew the attention of a warrior." Niro was still not happy about that.

"Robin, you should never go anywhere without Niro. When you are joined you may walk around more freely." Kelila stopped and looked down at Robin. "Plus there are dangers other than just horny warriors."

"I understand." Robin replied.

"Don't worry I disciplined her." Niro added.

Robin couldn't help but smiling thinking about his form of punishment. "What is that big building over there?" Robin pointed at the larger building off to the side by itself.

"This is where the weaker males are kept." Niro said as though he was disgusted by it. "I don't have need for it."

"Weaker males?" Robin concluded this must be a hospital of some sort. She use to volunteer at the hospital back home, maybe she could do that here.

Justus Roux

"I must check the Trials staging grounds. You will come with me little one." Niro kissed his mother on the cheek then headed over to a large opened area.

"Like a sporting arena." Robin commented.

"Like hell!" Niro stopped abruptly and looked sternly at her.

"What did I say wrong?"

"No other male will be touching you." He growled.

"Oh wait a minute…. Sport doesn't mean the same thing it does here where I am from. "Robin thought for a moment. "Sport means events where men and women show their strength and speed."

"The games." Niro relaxed. "This is the Trial arena, a sport arena is somewhere you will never be, little one."

"What is a sport arena? I have to understand what that means so I don't make another blunder."

"Sport arena is where the winners of the Trials go to be pleasure by females given by protectors. It is an honor to have your female selected to be in the Sport arena." Niro pulled playfully on her braid. "You will not go to the sport arena."

Robin looked at the various gaming areas being set up. "This is for the sword." Niro pointed as they passed. "This for hand to hand." He grabbed her hand and pulled her closer to him as another warrior passed. "This is for Conja fight."

"What is a Conja?" Robin saw the big smile on Niro's face.

"I will show you Ducan." He looked like an excited boy as he led her to a very large stable.

Robin's eyes widen as she looked upon the creatures that resembled dragons. "This is Ducan." Niro stroked the scaly face of the creature. "These are trained Conjas Robin, wild ones are very dangerous so don't approach them."

"I don't plan on approaching this one."

"Come, Ducan will not hurt you." Niro gently placed Robin's hand on Ducan's snout. The scales were rough on her fingers. "He will be taking us to the Rundal's mountain."

"Oh goody." Robin really didn't want to fly across the land on this thing's back.

"Niro, small scouting troop at the border." A deep voice boomed. Robin backed up away from the door seeing the large barbarian sitting on the saddle back of one of the Conjas.

"Little one go back to the leader hut and find my father. He will protect you until I get back." Niro threw a saddle on Ducan's back. He watched Robin head out across the field toward the leader hut. His eyes didn't leave her until he saw her enter the hut. He wanted to escort her but there was little time. He would have to hurry to catch those Larmat warriors plus he wanted to hurry up and get back here to protect Robin. He had a bad feeling she wasn't doing what he told her to do.

Robin watched as Niro took to the air on the back of that dragon of his. About ten more warriors followed him. "Is he in any danger?" Robin asked when she smelt Kelila's familiar perfume.

"No, I pity any Larmat warrior dumb enough to challenge Niro. Now follow me I am sure Niro told you to go to his father." Kelila escorted Robin into Hakan's chamber.

He was sitting down at a large wooden table looking over what appeared to be maps. "Come here female." He growled.

"You have another female to guard for awhile." Kelila knew that growl; Hakan would have to wait to be fucked.

"Where is Niro?" Hakan said, looking up from the map.

"Taking care of the scouts."

"Stay in my sight little female." He went back to what he was doing.

"I will be in the bathing chamber." Kelila smiled over to Hakan. He watched her walk to the room just off of the chamber. He quickly stood up then looked down at Robin.

"Stay in this chamber." He grumbled then headed for the bathing chamber.

"Oh, I hate this why can't I look around." Robin went over to the map. She couldn't read it and had no idea what the heck she was looking at. Then the hospital popped into her mind. "Well…it wouldn't hurt to check on those weaker males at least I would be doing something useful."

She quietly stepped out of the chamber with all the noise coming from the bathing area she doubt they heard her. She looked down both ways of the hallway making sure no warriors were in sight. She did the same as she went outside. She now knew how a poor rabbit felt looking out for the wolf. She headed toward the large building having her eyes scanning the area the whole time.

Quietly she opened the large wooden doors. The smell of sweat and man were everywhere. This didn't have the antiseptic smell of a hospital. The sound of men grunting echoed through the room. Puzzled by this Robin slowly proceeded forward. Another set of doors were down the corridor she slowly opened those. There was a large opened area with several smaller chambers off to the side. Large pillars surrounded the area. Robin went over to one of the pillars and peeked into the middle of the large area. She couldn't believe what she saw and didn't know what to do now. So she stayed perfectly still.

A large warrior sat on a chair, he was completely naked. He was seated so his balls were hanging down from the chair. A small man laid on his back propped up on his elbows so he could lick at the warrior's balls. Robin watched the smaller man lick at a frantic pace as if he was terrified of something should he slow down. A second smaller man was kneeling beside the warrior sucking on the warrior's cock. The warrior held on to the man's head as he sucked.

Robin looked over to the side another warrior was standing up and thrusting at the wall, a pair of man's arms were wrapped around the warrior's hip, telling Robin the warrior was fucking this guy's mouth. Another warrior had a really skinny man bent over something as he fucked away at the guy's ass. Her attention went back to the warrior sitting down. He was grunting loudly as he held the man's head that was sucking his cock. He had handfuls of the man's hair bobbing him faster on his cock. The one who was licking his balls was still bathing every inch with fast, long strokes.

Robin froze, her heart pounded hard in her chest as her eyes locked with the large warrior who was sitting down. He grinned at her then pulled the man off his cock, stroked his cock a couple of times and spurted his cum all over the guy's face. The whole time his eyes never leaving

Robin's. He stood up and kicked the smaller man who had been licking his balls away from him. He reached down and grabbed his covering; his eyes still on Robin's. She watched as his cock grew hard again.

She gasped and started running when he charged at her. She raced through the hallway and straight out the door. She heard his heavy footsteps behind her as she hurried toward the leader hut. She reached out to push the door open but was lifted off her feet.

"Is that pussy all wet from watching?" He growled into her ear as his hand dug into her pussy. "Mmm, nice and wet." He carried her off to the side out of the view of the leader hut. He threw her to the ground then climbed on top of her. "You know how long it has been since I had some pussy." He pulled her covering up and forced her legs opened.

"Niro will kill you if you touch me!" She yelled pounding on his chest.

"He is welcome to try." With one quick movement he entered her. "You are so fucking tight." He moaned ramming more of his cock into her. "I am going to kill Niro and take this pussy for me." He growled thrusting faster.

Robin closed her eyes and thought of Niro. It was Niro who was taking her not this filthy barbarian who was grunting and sweating all over her. She felt him shutter and fall on her.

"I am going to fuck this pussy raw." He growled looking down at her.

"Get off her now!" Hakan's voice filled the gardens.

The warrior slowly pulled out and put his covering back on. He stood up and faced Hakan. "I will let Niro deal with you." He signaled to the three warriors and they took him away.

"Why did you leave the chamber?" Kelila wrapped Robin up in a new covering. Robin latched on to her. "Come inside." She helped Robin to her feet. She felt for the imported woman. Kelila had her share of this before she was joined. She carefully sat Robin on the bed and went over to get her something warm to drink.

"You disobeyed me." Hakan yelled. "Niro left you in my care and now you have been touched." He slammed his fist down on his desk causing the whole thing to rattle.

"Yelling at her will not help anything." Kelila handed Robin the warm liquid. "This is made from the bark of the Balma tree it will soothe you."

"Thank you." Robin sipped at the liquid it was actually pretty good, it tasted like a nice honey tea.

"Where did you go?" Kelila asked sitting next to her.

"I went to where the weaker males are."

"Why in the hell would you go there?" Hakan grumbled.

"I thought it was a hospital, you know a place for sick people." Robin sipped more of the tea.

"Arghh!" Hakan exclaimed leaving the room.

"Weaker males are males who are too weak or small to fight." Kelila moved Robin's hair out of her face. "They are used as females by warrior's who don't have a female."

"Just because they are smaller or weak they are treated like some sort of sex toy. What if they don't want to be?" Robin couldn't believe what she was hearing.

"Then they are forced to service the stronger male."

"That is not right." Robin set the cup down.

"No it isn't. But it is necessary. Now get some sleep before Niro comes home."

Chapter 7

Robin jerked awake upon hearing Niro's angry yell. The door burst open causing Robin to scoot up to the head of the bed. Niro fell to his knees and laid his head on the bed.

"I am sorry, little one." He said softly.

Robin hurried over to him and ran her hands through his hair. He slowly looked up into her eyes. "Did he hurt you?" He brought his hand to her face and cupped her cheek.

"I am alright."

"I failed you, little one." The sadness in his voice and eyes tore at Robin.

"No, Niro I disobeyed your father. It was my fault." Robin brought his head to her chest and wrapped her arms around his shoulders. Niro clung onto her.

"I swore another warrior would not touch you." His voice was very quiet and solemn.

Robin felt a warm sticky fluid in her hand as she ran it up his back. "Oh my God you are bleeding." She looked at her blood stained hand.

"It will heal." He pulled her closer to him. Imagines of the bastard fucking Robin filled his mind, breaking his heart. He was her protector he should have sent someone else after the scouts.

"We have to clean this, Niro." Robin tried to break free of his embrace but he wouldn't allow it. "It is not your fault, Niro. You didn't fail me."

"You are too kind little one." He buried his face in her breasts. She must think of him as a lesser warrior, he would never be good enough to join with her.

Robin ran her fingers through his hair trying to think of the right words to say. She closed her eyes and took in everything she had learned since she got here. "It is okay, Niro." She leaned her head against his. "We have to clean your wounds. How did you get this?" She saw the large cut on his back.

"I battled with the warrior who hurt you."

"What did you do to him?"

"I killed him of course. I may have failed you little one, but I have saved your name." He looked up into her eyes searching for anything that might tell him she still thought of him as the best warrior.

Robin ran her hands down his cheeks. Then the right words hit her, at least she hoped the right ones. "Then you are the better warrior." She smiled warmly at him when she saw his eyes light up.

"You honor me, little one." He ran his finger across her lips.

"Now can we clean your wound?" He released her and let her lead him to the bathing chamber.

Robin motioned for him to sit down on the stone bench. The whole room was warm and steamy. She gathered some cloths and went to him. Gently she wiped down the area but the gash was pretty deep. "You need stitches." She said holding the wash rag to the wound. "Wait here." She looked in every container and storage space looking for something that might help.

"Little one, use this." Niro handed her a string like substance and a very sharp needle.

"Sit back down." She ordered pointing at the stone bench. Niro smiled at her and did what she said. "What can I use so this won't hurt you?"

"Just mend me, little one, I will endure the pain."

"I don't want to hurt you."

"I have had far worse, it is okay."

Robin reluctantly started to stitch up his wound. She knew it must have hurt terribly but Niro never made a sound or flinched. After a few moments she was done.

She grabbed a large bowl and filled it with the hot water from the pool. She placed a fresh cloth in it then went back to where Niro was sitting. She sat the bowl down by his feet then reached up and unfastened his covering.

"You want sport." Niro stroked her hair.

"I am going to bathe you." She started at his feet then slowly and softly worked her way up. Niro watched the gentle way she bathed him, her hands caressing and exploring every inch of him. He bit his lip trying to restrain himself when she cupped his balls and stroked his cock with the cloth. Her hands journeyed up caressing and bathing every muscle line of his wide chest. She slowly rose to her feet and grabbed another water basin and put fresh water in the one she had been using. She went behind him and freed his long hair from its leather tie. She buried her hands in the wealth of his soft hair as he leaned his head back resting against her. She stepped aside and tilted his head back. She let the warm water run down his hair, her fingers worked the soap through massaging his scalp. Niro closed his eyes and enjoyed the tenderness of this moment.

"Better make sure you are rinsed off good." Robin whispered in his ear. She walked over to the large bathing pool and removed her covering then stepped inside the pool.

Niro walked over to her and went inside the pool as well. He pulled her to him reaching behind her and freeing her hair from the braid. Robin looked deep into his eyes as his fingers went through her hair. Slowly he lowered his lips to hers. His kiss was gentle and unhurried.

"I must bathe you, little one." Niro whispered against her lips. He grabbed the water pitcher that was beside the pool and filled it up. He tilted her head back and poured the water onto her hair. His fingers worked through every strand of her hair, his touch soft. When he was done he lifted her up and sat her on the side of the pool. He reached for a cloth and starting at her feet he began to bathe her. His tongue followed the cloth.

"Niro." Robin sighed when his tongue ran up the length of her inner thigh. Her eyes followed every movement of his mouth. He looked up into her eyes as he blew gently onto her pussy lips. "Niro." She said holding her breath. She could feel the warmth of his breath on her pussy. He ran his tongue up one of her pussy lips then the other.

"Please, Niro." Her breathing more labored. She reached down and pushed his face closer to her pussy unable to take his sweet torture anymore. Niro growled and lapped feverishly at her clit. She responded by grinding her pussy against his tongue. His mouth latched onto her clit and he began to nurse on it.

"Niro, yes...." Her hands tightened in his hair as she pushed his face deeper into her pussy. The sucking sensation on her clit felt so wonderful, Robin laid back on

Protector of My Heart

the stone floor spreading her legs wider as her orgasm hit. Niro growled again when he felt her clit pulsing in his mouth. He lapped at the opening wanting to drink down all her sweet nectar. His tongue darted in and out coaxing more of her sweetness out.

"Niro, please…please I need your cock. Oh God please Niro!" Robin yelled out.

Niro pulled her to him and she wrapped her legs around his waist. She moaned feeling his hard cock fill her pussy completely. "Ride me, fucking ride me." He howled.

Both worked in a harmonious rhythm as his cock drove in and out of her. Robin wrapped tightly around him pulling him as close as he could be. She wanted the hardness of his male body against her as his cock thrust into her over and over. Niro wrapped his arms around her pulling her to him, wanting her softness against him, wanting her warm breath on his skin while his cock was surrounded by her warm wet heat.

"Niro!!" Robin screamed as the orgasm took over her body. She heard his howl as he took his pleasure. She laid her head against his chest still holding on to him tightly. She felt his strong arms pulling her closer. Being surrounded by his embrace made her safe and warm. He held her like that until she let him go.

Justus Roux

Chapter 8

Robin watched Niro strapping his knife to his thigh. She felt her pussy growing wetter watching his thigh muscles flex. She had a sudden urge to run her tongue all over that strong thigh.

"Mmm, little one I like the way you are looking at me."

Her eyes shot up to his face that sexy smile of his made her even wetter. "Do you think we have time for some quick sport?" Robin stood up on the bed and let her covering fall from her body. She squealed when Niro grabbed her and pinned her up against the wall. He quickly undid his covering then rammed his cock into her pussy. Robin felt his sword against his back. Her leg rubbed up against the hilt of the knife that was strapped to his thigh. The urgency of their lovemaking made it that much hotter. The feeling of his strong body against hers, the sounds he made heighten her pleasure. Her orgasm hit quick and hard making her whole body shutter. When she opened her eyes he was looking into her face, taking delight in watching her pleasure.

"Keep looking at me Niro." She said as she watched the pleasure wash across his face. She felt his body press into hers, felt his cock pulse deep inside her giving her a since of satisfaction. Enjoying his pleasure more than her own.

"We must ready for the Trial." Niro slowly pulled out of her then gently set her on the ground.

"So is this like an all day thing?" Robin wrapped her covering on.

"Yes, you will stay by my side, understand?" Niro said fastening his covering back on.

"Aren't you going to compete in this Trial?"

"No, I am a protector there is no need for me to compete." Niro tightened the metal bracelets on his arm. He ran his hand over the left one; he hoped someday soon Robin would be wearing it.

"Okay I am lost again. So you are a protector. I don't think someone will be stupid enough to touch me with you right there."

"How do I explain this?" Niro sat down on the bed; he kept forgetting that Robin wasn't from Malka. "The Trial is for males to prove they are worthy to become protectors."

"Worthy?"

"Oh yes, a male must prove he is a better warrior. This is done either by battle or by winning the Trials. Only the strongest males are worthy of a female."

"If this is the case, why haven't you been a female's protector earlier? I mean you have won this Trial two years in a row. And everyone keeps telling me how good you are in battle. I would think this would most certainly prove you are worthy."

"I have not found a female I wanted to pledge myself to." Niro quickly stood up. Sharing his feelings made him feel very uncomfortable and he wanted to end this conversation now. "We must get to the Trial."

Protector of My Heart

"But you are my protector." Robin looked to the ground. "Did you only do this because your father wanted it?" She knew there was a catch somewhere. She didn't know why she was getting all upset, after all she barely knew the guy.

Niro went over to her and fell to his knees in front of her. He placed his hands gently on her thighs and took a moment to compose himself. "My father wanted me to bring you back that was all. You were going to be given to the winner of the Trial." Niro brought his hand up to the loose strands of hair that framed her face. "But I wanted to be your protector, so I claim the right."

"Why?"

"You warm my heart. You did the first moment I laid eyes on you."

"Niro." A deep voice called out.

Niro leaned forward and covered Robin's body while glaring at the large warrior who dared to step foot in his chambers.

"I do not wish to challenge you." The warrior kept his eyes to the ground. "Your father wishes to speak with you."

"Alright, now leave." Niro grumbled. "Come, little one, let's go." Niro waited a moment, waited for her to say the words back, but she only got up and straightened her covering. He still hasn't proven to her what a great warrior he is. If he had she would have said the words back.

Robin sensed something was wrong with Niro as they walked silently to Hakan's chambers. "Stay with my mother." Niro quietly said as he went into the adjacent room.

"Hello Robin are you excited to see the Trials?" Kelila said offering Robin a chair next to her.

"Yeah, I am. "

"You don't seem all that excited."

"I think I said or did something wrong and I am not sure what." Robin kept looking at the door Niro went into.

"Tell me what happen and I will try to help."

"I was asking Niro about the Trial and he explained to me they were basically to prove who the strongest warrior was. Now if I understood right this gives the winner the right to be a protector."

"Yes, you got that part right or he can prove himself in battle."

"Yeah that is what Niro said."

"Since there are so few females having them join with the strongest warriors will insure strong children."

"Okay I guess that makes sense. I asked Niro why he didn't become a protector before now; you know seeing how he has proven himself and all."

"Believe me, Robin, I wondered that myself. But when he said he wanted to wait for a female who warmed his heart. Well, let's say a mother couldn't be more proud."

"Warmed his heart, what does that mean."

"Do you not have this where you are from?"

"I don't understand what that is supposed to mean."

"Let me explain. I have been joined to Hakan for many years when I look upon him he warms my heart. Do you understand? Let me put this another way, your male back on your planet, since he was your mate, did he not warm your heart."

Robin thought for a moment and then her hand went up to her heart. *"You warm my heart. You did the first moment I laid eyes on you."* Niro's words repeated in her

Protector of My Heart

mind. The door opened from the other room and Niro stormed out.

"What has happened?" Kelila hurried over to Niro.

"Niro, it will be the grandest honor and will show your warmth for the people of Dascon." Hakan said following Niro into the room.

"Come, little one." Niro looked over at her and became puzzled her hand was clutching her heart and she looked white as a ghost. Niro hurried over to her. "What is wrong, little one?" His hand felt all over her body looking for any kind of injury.

"I love you too, Niro. I really do. "

"Love? What is this love?" Niro's hands went to her face and gently stroked. His poor little one must had a delayed response to being used by that other warrior. He would make it better.

"You warm my heart, Niro." Robin fought to keep the tears back and prayed to God she was right and that phrase did mean I love you, in Malka terms.

"Little one…" Niro kissed at her whole face his heart about to burst with emotion. He looked deep into her eyes. She was a fast learner and was trying so hard to learn about Malka. She shouldn't have to forget everything about her world. "Then I love you, Robin." He stumbled over the words hoping he phrased it right and above all hoping that meant the same thing as warm my heart. When he saw the tears roll down her face and the large smile, he knew it did. He gently wiped the tears away then stood up and faced his father.

"I will not allow Robin to be the prize for the winner of the Trials." Niro glared into his father's face.

"I am afraid you have no choice my son. What is done is done, my word stands."

"Ahh!!!!" Niro yelled drawing his sword.

Hakan just stood there. "I will not battle with you my son."

"Niro!" Kelila ran over to him. "Sheath your sword! How dare you challenge the leader of Dascon." She gently placed her hand on his wrist urging him to do what she said.

"Damn you." Niro growled at his father then he sheathed his sword. "Would you have let mother been the prize?"

"He did before we were joined Niro." Kelila said. Niro just stood there looking at his father.

"Did you think I enjoyed the thought of another warrior touching her? But if I was unwilling to share the prize of my heart, what right did I have to ask others. Our males need something Niro. One day I hope to be done with this, that our females are safe to walk on their own. But for now I have no choice but to continue with the traditions. So don't you dare think what I asked of you that I asked lightly. "

"Come, little one." Niro grabbed Robin roughly by the arm and pulled her to her feet then they left the room.

"I am pleased you didn't challenge your son." Kelila wrapped her arms around Hakan.

"He would have won if I had."

Kelila looked up into her mate's face. Never had Hakan turned down a challenge before. Niro would have to someday challenge his father to become leader of Dascon. She knew now Hakan was ready to let Niro take over for him. But the thought of her mate yielding to anyone's sword, even her own son's sword was not something she wanted to ever think about.

Protector of My Heart

Robin followed Niro out to the Trial grounds there were hundreds of warriors all over the field. The sound of metal clashing, male war cries and the shrill growl of the Conja filled the air.

"These events are fast." Niro said to her. She struggled to take it all in. She spotted a couple of Rundal in the audience. She saw females with their mates and protectors, small children staying close to their mothers. Wagons carrying food and drink worked their way around the grounds.

"Come little one." Niro slowly headed up to a large platform where Hakan and Kelila had emerged. Niro led her up the stairs of the platform then took a seat next to his mother. His hand tightened on Robin's when Hakan stood up.

"Warriors of Dascon." Hakan cried out. A hush fell over the entire field. "Today you prove how hard you have trained. Today you prove yourselves warriors."

Robin watched as Niro stood up and joined in with the other males in their battle cry. Two women came up onto the platform. Niro looked down at Robin and gently helped her up.

"You must be presented." He said in a solemn voice. Robin could see in his eyes just how much this was tearing him up. She took a deep breath then walked up to the other two women.

"These females will be the prizes for the winner." Hakan moved to the first dark-haired one. "Winner of sword." He moved to the next. "Winner of strength." Hakan moved to Robin, "The female of Niro is for the grand warrior." Apparently the warriors approved of

Hakan's choice, the growling and howling rang up. "On with the Trials."

Robin looked back at Niro; he stood up and opened his arms she rushed over to him. "It is only for one night, little one." Niro nuzzled his chin on the top of her head. "Then no other warrior will ever touch you again."

Niro looked out over the field. He wondered which one would be grand warrior and more importantly could he beat this man in battle. A growl escaped him when he saw Demos step on to the sword field. Demos was a skilled warrior, Niro had fought many battles along side of Demos.

Robin followed Niro's eyes. She watched the large warrior who was about the size of Niro, his hair was a rich brown color and it hung down the length of his back. This man dominated the other warrior quickly. Robin backed up a bit, this man was gorgeous, but one of his eyes had a large scar running down it, the other eye was a brilliant violet color. "I take it you don't like him." Robin asked Niro.

"Demos is a very skilled warrior." Niro really hoped Demos didn't become grand warrior. He wasn't sure he could win a challenge with him, if Demos decided he wanted Robin.

Niro watched Robin more than he watched the warriors. He answered every question she had. He tried everything not to thing about Robin being in the arms of another warrior tonight. He also watched Demos who so far dominated the Trials.

"Demos will win." Saa said as he stood by Niro. Saa had his arm firmly around Sabrina and she seemed most comfortable there.

"Looks that way." Niro quickly replied.

Protector of My Heart

"You are a better warrior than Demos is." Saa said giving Niro a firm pat on the back. "Sabrina wants to watch the Conja match."

"Come with us you two." Sabrina added.

"Can we Niro?"

Niro saw the excited look in Robin's eyes how could he deny such a small request. "Come, little one." Niro gently grabbed her hand and led her out to the Conja field.

"Would you look at that." Sabrina exclaimed watching the warriors fighting with one another on the backs of the large conjas. The shrill cry of the animals pierced the ears when their rider was struck.

"You fight like that?" Robin said to Niro. She gasped watching one of the riders fall from his animal landing on the ground with a thump.

"Yes, but I don't fall off my Conja." Niro purred into her ear.

"Full of yourself aren't you." She playfully punched at his chest.

Niro laughed hard then grabbed two mugs of drink off the cart. He handed one to Robin. She watched him drink it first. She looked in the mug and grimace at the green slimy liquid that was in it.

"Drink up female." Niro slapped her on the ass.

"What is it?" She stuck her tongue out at the idea of drinking such a god awful smelling drink.

"Pipom."

"Well the name is fitting."

"It makes for good mood." Niro smiled at her with the one she would do anything he asked her to do.

She closed her eyes and took a swallow of the drink. Surprisingly it tasted heavenly. It was sweet and tart at the same time. "This is pretty good." Robin said taking another big swallow of it.

"Whoa, you must drink slowly." Niro took the mug from her. "To much and you will end up like him." He pointed over to a large warrior passed out over by a large Balma tree.

"Oh." Robin sure didn't need to be all drunk tonight.

"Wow, he looks like a strong one." Sabrina commented as Demos climbed onto his conja's saddle. Saa growled and pulled Sabrina closer. "You know we really got to work on this jealousy thing."

Niro watched Robin as she looked at the match. She was impressed by Demos' skill he could see it in her face. Niro had to fight the urge to jump into the ring and take Demos down.

"Damn that guy can ride that thing good. Did you see him knock that dude off in like what a minute." Sabrina smiled and clapped for Demos as he left the field.

"AHH!!" Saa roared as he smashed the food cart.

"What?" Sabrina stepped away from him.

"You honor another warrior in front of me." He rumbled.

"Sorry Mr. Touchy geez. What is so wrong about giving the guy a compliment?" Sabrina jumped back when Saa smashed his fist into the food cart again.

"You are stating Demos is a better warrior than Saa." Niro said.

"Oh no Saa baby, you are a much better warrior than that old Demos over there. Hell I bet you could knock him off the…the funny looking lizard thing even quicker. I mean damn look at you." Sabrina wrapped her arms around his arm. "You are so big and strong, my big bad warrior man." Sabrina smiled up at him. He grunted and stood there with a smile on his face. Sabrina looked at Robin. "Not much different than earth, huh."

Robin started laughing uncontrollably. "What is so funny?" Niro asked.

"You wouldn't understand." Both women said still laughing.

ଓଓଓଓ

Robin felt funny as the two women wrapped a golden covering around her. Niro had left the staging area; he couldn't take watching her being handed over to Demos.

"Don't be frightened." One said softly to her. "It is an honor to be prize for grand warrior."

"I don't feel so honored." Robin still had Niro's face in her mind. That look of sheer agony as he looked at her one more time when he left the staging area.

"You are so small. I hope Demos doesn't hurt you." The very large dark-haired woman stated snotty.

"Hey you can have Demos."

"How dare you even think of disgracing Niro." The woman almost growled at her.

"I don't plan on disgracing him, he-woman."

"My name is Eudora and I would sooner kill you then see you joined with Niro."

Robin watched as the other woman left the room leaving her alone with Eudora. "Hey listen, in case you haven't notice your land is running over with gorgeous warrior guys. So there is plenty to go around." Robin sure the hell didn't want to fight with the amazonian woman.

Justus Roux

"Niro is the best warrior and deserves a female such as me."

Robin backed away as the woman moved closer. "Eudora, what are you doing?" Robin was never so relieved to hear Kelila's voice.

"Making sure this puny female was ready for Demos."

"You may go now I will finish dressing her."

Eudora looked at Robin as though she was some disease and stomped from the room. "Be careful of her." Kelila said.

"That is an understatement."

"Eudora has tried for many years to capture Niro's attention."

"I thought it was something like that." Robin wrapped her arms around herself.

"You are shaking." Kelila put her arm around Robin. "If Niro hasn't hurt you Demos surely won't."

"I am not worried about that so much. I just don't want to be with him."

"I understand what you feel." Kelila led Robin out of the room. "When I waited for the winner of the Trial to claim me, I was terrified. I felt like I was betraying Hakan's heart." Kelila bowed her head at the two guards. "But if I refused to let the winner claim me I would dishonor the one male that held my heart. This I would never do. So I did what I must and allowed the winner to do with me as he would. For it was only one night but the shame I would of brought Hakan would have lasted for years if I refused." Kelila stopped at the door to the guest chamber. "Do you understand?"

"Yes. I will not shame Niro." Robin took a deep breath and entered the chamber.

Protector of My Heart

Kelila waited by the door to make sure Robin didn't change her mind. Even though Kelila was quite fond of Robin, she wouldn't allow anyone to bring shame to her son.

෴෴෴

Robin walked slowly into the chamber, she saw Demos standing at the far end of it watching her every move. He was even bigger in this small chamber. The closer she got to him the more afraid she became. His body was one solid wall of muscles. He had to be blind in the one eye because the scar runs right over it. His other eye a brilliant violet color and it seemed to pierce into Robin. He was dressed just like Niro had been except the metal bracelets he wore had different symbols on it.

"You are most beautiful." His voice was the deepest voice Robin had ever heard before.

"Thank you." Robin looked down at the floor. She could hear his heavy footsteps coming closer.

"Niro is lucky." Demos gently placed his hand on her shoulder and allowed his hand to go down her arm. "I will try to be gentle."

"Thank you." Robin slowly looked up to his face as he untied her wrapping. She heard him groan once her body was exposed to him. She gasped when he lifted her up so his hungry mouth could reach her nipples.

"You are so soft." He mumbled as he sucked on her nipple. His hands groped at her ass, kneading and squeezing. He held her up as though she weighed nothing. He carried her to the bed. Robin braced herself to be thrown into the bed, like Niro seemed to like to do, but was surprised when Demos gently laid her down.

"I wasn't going to take you, out of respect for Niro...." He sucked hard on her nipple as he laid more of his weight on her. "But I can't stop myself I must take you."

Robin grabbed a hold of the furs on the bed as he entered her. His cock stretched her too quickly and caused her discomfort. She felt him pull out and lower his head down between her legs. "I will get you ready for my cock." He lapped at her pussy concentrating on her clit. His tongue moved in long hard strokes over her clit in the same rhythm same pressure. Robin felt her orgasm build; she tried to fight not wanting to take pleasure from this. How could she when Niro was in so much pain. But Demos' tongue hit all the right spots. Robin grabbed a handful of his soft dark-brown hair as her orgasm hit so strong she cried out from it.

"You are ready for me now." He said as he climbed back on her and entered her. The warmth and tightness of her pussy felt so good. It has been to long since he was with a female. He was so into the pleasure she was giving him he didn't hear her cries of pain.

Robin hit Demos' chest as hard as she could. His grip on her hips was too tight and the pain was getting to be too much to bear.

Demos released her hips then quickly turned her over. He lowered her upper body down and lifting her hips up to him. "Please don't take me like this." Robin sobbed this felt wrong only Niro had the right to take her like this. She couldn't help but feel this way.

She felt Demos roll her over and entered her again. He sat back on the bed and pulled her up so now she was facing him. "Ride me." He growled. His voice so low it scared her making her obey him. She wrapped her legs around him and slid her pussy up and down on his cock as he kneaded her ass and grinded her hips into him.

He wanted to bite her, bend her over and take her the way a protector would. He couldn't, not with her sobbing. He gripped her ass tighter and drove his cock deeper into her. "Give me my pleasure." He let her go and grabbed a hold of the edge of the bed. He closed his eyes and leaned back letting her ride him to orgasm. Her pussy milked every last drop of cum from his body as he fell back into the bed and enjoyed the sensations that raced through him.

෴෴෴

Niro paced up and down the hallway. Imagines of Robin and Demos mating filled his mind igniting his anger. "AHHHH!!!" He yelled drawing his sword.

"Come Niro, spar with me."

"Saa, I am liable to hurt you at this moment."

"Afraid I will shame you." Saa quickly blocked the blow of Niro's sword. His hand vibrated from the impact.

He sparred with Niro until he tired. Both men leaned up against the wall all worn out. "It is only one night but it must feel like an eternity." Saa said sliding down to the ground.

"I can't stop thinking about them together." Niro sat down next to Saa. "I want to break or kill something. I want to fight until I pass out from being tired."

"Well in that case I will round up some more sparring partners for you." Saa pulled himself up.

"Where is Sabrina?" Niro asked.

"I locked her in my chambers. She is sleeping."

"Thank you Saa."

Saa nodded and headed out to find more warriors to spar with Niro. He wouldn't know how to get through this night if Sabrina was laying with another warrior.

Chapter 9

Robin woke up her body so sore she could barely move. Demos fucked her so much and in so many ways except for the way a protector would. He respected that.

"Niro is a lucky male." Demos ran his fingers through her tousled hair. "I will tell Hakan you have honored Niro." He strapped on his sword then gently stroked her cheek. He looked at her for a moment then walked out of the chamber.

Robin slowly got out of bed and headed for the bathing chamber. The warm steam hit her waking her up. She carefully stepped into the hot water and let it soothe her tired body. Demos looked like a harden man but his touches told a different story. If she was distressed about something he wouldn't do it. Robin wrung out the water from the cloth letting the droplets run down her arm. Niro looked like a fierce warrior but his touches were gentle. Though of course he could be quite rough, this made Robin smile, she rather enjoyed his roughness. She wrapped her arms around herself, but she cherished his gentleness.

"Are you okay?"

"Sabrina, Saa let you walk around by yourself?"

"The big oaf is waiting just outside the chamber. May I join you? The water looks so inviting."

"Of course." The bathing pool was rather large. Robin has grown to love soaking in them.

"Did Demos hurt you?" Sabrina slowly lowered herself into the water.

"No, he didn't." Robin went back to bathing herself.

"You know I shouldn't really tell you this, but I sure the hell would love to hear this about Saa."

Robin stopped what she was doing and gave her full attention to Sabrina. "Well what is it?"

"Okay you beat it out of me. Niro was so upset about you and Demos that he fought something like twenty warriors last night. He kept fighting until he was so tired that Saa had to help him to his chamber." Sabrina started washing herself. "He has got it bad for you girl."

"I got to go to him." Robin climbed out of the bath even though every muscle in her body still ached.

"Could you tell Saa to come in here? I need someone to wash my back." Saa had told Sabrina to tell Robin about Niro. He knew Robin would go to Niro before he had a chance to wake up.

"Of course." Robin wrapped her covering around herself and headed out of the chamber. "Sabrina wants you to wash her back." Robin said to Saa as she passed him. She heard him hurry into the chamber. She quickly made her way down the hall, straight toward Niro's chamber. She quietly opened the door and saw him sleeping in his big bed.

"Niro." She whispered sitting down into the bed. Her hand gently went down his bare back. Her fingers tracing every muscle line as her eyes followed.

"Little one." Niro rolled over and opened his arms to her. Robin fell into his embrace, holding him tightly.

"Never again." He rubbed his face against the top of her head. "I will never let another warrior touch you again." He lifted her face up to his and kissed her lips softly. He rolled her over and got on top of her. He needed to make love to her, needed to get his scent on her.

"Niro, I am sorry I just can't right now."

Niro rolled off her and begun checking her for injuries. Demos better not have hurt her. If so much as one bruise was on her skin.

"I am just a bit sore. I will be okay later then I will show you how much I missed you." Robin reached up and pulled him back down to her. "Let me just hold you for awhile."

Niro wrapped his arm around her waist and laid his head on her breasts. "You warm my heart, little one."

"I love you too, Niro." Robin ran her fingers through his long dark hair and simply enjoyed being so close to him.

Justus Roux

Protector of My Heart

Chapter 10

"Malin, one of the scouts has made it back alive." Rasmus said as he entered the royal chamber.

"Can you not see I am having my cock sucked on?" Malin pushed the woman's head down forcing more of his cock into her mouth. He looked up at Rasmus and smiled when the woman made a gagging noise. "There is a free end you may use it." Malin was the leader of the Larmat and Rasmus was his best warrior. Rasmus quickly undid his covering and got behind the woman. Both men were very muscular and both had blonde hair. Their golden hair is what marked them part of the Larmat. Malin had intense blue eyes that could pierce right through someone, where as Rasmus had one blue and one green eye. "Come on fuck the bitch, make that pussy bleed." Malin growled as he thrust violently into the woman's mouth. He laid back in the bed and spread his legs open wide as he bobbed the woman's head faster on his cock. "Come on suck on me, female." He grinded the woman's head against him; he could feel Rasmus brutally ramming his cock into her. He held the woman's head to him and watched as Rasmus roared out his orgasm. He closed his eyes and relished the feeling of his own orgasm.

"I believe she has passed out Malin." Rasmus said noticing the woman had stopped struggling.

Malin slowly opened his eyes and then pulled his cock from the woman's mouth. She gasped for air as she coughed rolling onto the other side of the bed. "Take this Dascon slut away." Malin motioned to the two guards standing by the chamber door. He stood up and put back on his covering. "Tell me what did the scout had to report."

Rasmus put back on his covering and grabbed the mug of pipom from Malin. "Niro has become a protector."

"Really?"

"It was one of the females the Rundal had provided for them."

"Damn Rundal, we would have taken over the Dascon by now if it wasn't for them."

"I didn't get to much information from the scout because he didn't live long enough. Demos' blade cut him deep."

"That fucking Demos..." Malin paced around in the room. Hakan was good at predicting his every move. Malin wanted to wipe out those damn Rundal, but Hakan was not easy to get around. "This was all the scout said."

"Yes, I am afraid so."

"Damn." Malin paced around. Why hasn't Niro killed Hakan yet, after all Malin had killed his own father two years ago, why wait to rule. Malin abruptly stopped. "Rasmus, what would make a Dascon warrior risk coming into Larmat territory?"

"Glory?"

"No, no... those damn Dascon warriors would do anything for their females." Malin smiled widely. "We need to get Niro's female then he will come to me."

"As so will the rest of the Dascon warriors."

Protector of My Heart

"Oh no, Niro will not waste time rounding up other warriors, he would want his female back." Malin took another big gulp of his drink. "Would you want your female left alone with a Larmat warrior?" Malin chuckled.

"But how do we get his female? He will be around her at all times."

"Post scouts around the village of Dascon and around the Rundal village. Sooner or later his female will want to explore her new world then we will have her. Give orders for no one to kill Niro, I just want his female."

"As you wish." Rasmus said leaving the room.

Malin grabbed his sword and headed for the training grounds. His mind thinking of all the nasty things he will do with Niro's female and how good it will feel to run his blade through the son of Hakan.

Justus Roux

Chapter 11

"Do we have to ride this thing to the Rundal Mountain?" Robin tried to fight with Niro as he placed her on the saddle of Ducan.

"It is the fastest and safest way, little one. Now stop squirming or Ducan is liable to bite you." Niro laughed loudly when Robin instantly stopped moving.

"What is so funny?" She playfully punched at Niro's shoulder. Ducan let out a shrill cry. "Only joking, see he is not hurt at all." Robin gently rubbed Niro's shoulder as she looked into Ducan's eyes.

"I am afraid Ducan is very protective of me." Niro petted the animal on the snout then climbed on the saddle behind Robin. He wrapped one of his arms around her waist and held onto the reins with his other hand.

"Oh I know I am not going to like this." Robin grabbed Niro's arm and held on for dear life as Ducan flapped his large wings. Robin could feel them lifting off the ground. She heard Niro growl so she looked to her side and saw Demos and two other warriors riding their conjas.

"Escorts?" Robin asked.

"They always accompany me whenever I go to the Rundal." Niro couldn't look over at Demos; he didn't want to see if Demos was looking at Robin.

"Whoa look at this." Robin exclaimed making Niro forget his jealousy for a moment. They were soaring high in the sky now, giving them a good view of the surrounding area.

"Beautiful isn't it?" Niro said pulling Robin closer.

"It's beyond that." Robin's eyes looked everywhere. The natural beauty of this planet was breath taking. There were no highways, power lines, billboards or tons of buildings cluttering up everything. The Balma trees gave brilliance to the landscape. Strange birds fluttered everywhere. The mountain range just beyond looked as though it was a painting and gave real character to the landside.

Niro looked at his world through Robin's wonderment. He saw the beauty that for so long he had taken for granted. "We will camp just outside of the Rundal village, it will be night soon and we don't want to be in the skies then."

"Why not?"

"Wild conja come out at night."

"Then shouldn't we go into the village?"

"Rundal close up the village at dusk. It is for their safety." Niro pulled on the reins signaling to Ducan to land. He wished they would have left sooner, so they would have made the Rundal village on time. Being out in the open so close to the mountain range was not the safest thing. The Larmat scouts he chased were weighing heavy on his mind. Malin was up to something but he couldn't get out of the scouts what.

Ducan landed gently in a clearing. Demos and the two warriors followed suit. Niro helped Robin off of Ducan and set her gently on the ground. "Do not wander too far." Niro said sternly.

Protector of My Heart

"I can help with something, you know like gather fire wood." Robin said.

"You will stay close to Ducan and wait for me to set up camp." Niro gestured to the two warriors and they headed off into the forest. Demos was already setting up the tents. Niro took a deep breath and try to shake off the jealousy. He knew he would have to find away around this, after all Demos was one of the best warriors he had.

Robin stood there watching the men ready things. She hated not being able to help. Ducan laid down and closed his eyes. Robin decided she would help with the fire wood. She walked a little ways into the woods looking for small branches and twigs that would be useful. She managed to gather up an armful of twigs then turned around headed straight back the way she came. "What is that smell?" A sulfuric odor was strong in the air. Quickly she looked around. She dropped the armful of twigs when she caught sight of the large conja that was staring at her. "Oh god please let that be Ducan." This blackish colored female conja Robin didn't remember seeing. "What do I do?" If she ran it would surely catch her. Maybe if she stand still it wouldn't see her.

Niro finished putting up the last tent. He went over to Ducan to collect Robin the sooner she was out of sight the better he would feel. When he got to Ducan Robin was nowhere in sight. His heart pounded loudly in alarm. "Robin!!" He called out.

"Niro, help me!!!"

He moved quickly toward Robin's scream. He drew his sword ready to kill whatever dared to threaten his female. "Don't move!" Niro's voice boomed causing the conja to turn toward him. "Slowly back away, little one." Niro closed in on the large beast.

Justus Roux

"Don't you dare fight that thing." The conja's head snapped back toward Robin.

"Don't make a sound." Niro slowly inched toward the beast. He let out his battle cry causing the beast to back up. It snarled and hissed at him clearly challenging him.

"Slowly head back to camp, little one and don't say a word."

Robin couldn't move, she was more afraid for Niro than for herself at the moment. She held her breath as she watched him charge at the large beast. He dodged the beast's claw. She couldn't just stand here and let him fight that beast alone. She ran out of the forest. She saw the other two warriors go the wrong way. She would never reach them in time. "Demos!" Robin yelled seeing him standing there with his sword drawn trying to figure out which way to go to find Niro. "This way." She went back into the forest and hoped that Demos had followed her.

Robin screamed when the beast's claws almost got her. She felt herself being pushed to the ground. "Little one, I said go back to camp." Niro covered her with his body.

"Niro watch out!" Robin yelled seeing the beast's claw heading right toward him. The beast yelled in pain when Demos' sword sliced off one of its talons. Niro quickly jumped to his feet and helped Demos finish the beast off.

Robin ran into Niro's arms and held him as tightly as she could. "Thank you Demos." Niro said holding Robin tightly to him.

"You have done the same for me Niro many times." Demos sheathed his sword and headed back to camp.

Protector of My Heart

"I am sorry Niro. I know I should have listened to you." Robin held him tighter. "You could have been killed, because of me."

"Shh, I am happy that you are not hurt." Niro picked Robin up into his arms and carried her back to camp. "We must get into the tent. We don't want to be out here in the dark." Niro set her down by the tent. Robin couldn't help but notice that the tent seemed to be made of animal skin.

"You know this feels like Ducan, well if he had dry skin."

"It is a skin from a conja; it will keep us safe from them for they don't attack their own." Niro gestured for Robin to get into the tent.

"What animal does all this fur come from?" Robin said running her hand through the fur that was laid out on the floor.

"From the Bamk and…

"That horse like thingy from earlier?"

"Yes and some fur comes from the trof. Most animals don't have much fur; there is no need for it."

"A trof, I am almost afraid to see it."

"It lives on the mountain along with the Bamk. It is much cooler up in the mountains, so you will have to wear an extra covering."

"You were so brave to take on the conja." Robin let her eyes wander over his glorious body.

"You were in danger. I would have killed anything that threatened you." Niro finished closing up the tent. He looked over at Robin. His cock grew instantly hard just by that look on her face. "You enjoy looking at me?" Niro had no idea females enjoyed watching males as much as males liked watching them.

Justus Roux

"Oh, very much so."

"What is so good about my body? I look like any other warrior."

"Come here and I will show you what I like about your body." Robin pulled her covering off. She brought her hands to her breasts and slowly let her hands caress them, letting her fingers roll over her nipples. "Lay down, Niro." She said with her sexiest voice.

Niro quickly removed his covering and laid down on the furs. "Where should I start?" Robin moved down to his feet. "My what big feet you have." She massaged his foot then pressed his foot against her breasts, allowing her nipples to rub between his toes.

"My cock is hungry for you, little one." Niro growled.

"Well it will have to wait its turn won't it." Robin let her hands travel up his calves and thighs. "I love how hard your body feels under my hands." She slowly spread his legs and started licking his inner thighs. Robin deliberately skipped his cock deciding to save the best part for last. "Mmm, your body is so hard. I love these muscle lines." Her tongue followed her fingers as she traveled up his chest. Her hands rubbed his shoulders. "You are so broad and strong." She allowed her breast to hang just above his mouth.

"Female…" He growled raising his mouth to her nipple.

"Ah ah, I am not done yet." She rubbed her wet pussy down his chest and pressed her whole body against his.

"Stop teasing me with the softness of your pussy…."

"Shh, I am not done. " She brought her fingers to his lips. "These lips feel and taste so good."

Niro sucked on her finger. Robin leaned over and kissed him, long, hot and wet. "Your face is so handsome." She whispered against his lips. "And your eyes are so beautiful, so green, so alive."

"No more teasing female." Niro started to growl like an animal.

Robin sat up then let her pussy rub down his body until she was straddling his leg. Her mouth hovered over his cock as she looked up into his eyes. "No more teasing." He growled tangling his hands in her hair. He pushed down on her head thrusting his cock up. Robin allowed him to guide her head. She sucked as hard as she could. Niro's thrusts became harder as he bobbed her head on his cock. "You teased me to long, damn it." He growled thrusting harder in her mouth.

Robin felt his cock going further down her throat, his hands pulling on her hair. His growling became more animalistic as his thrusts became harder. Robin tried to break free from his grasp, surely he would allow her to get up but she became alarmed when he wouldn't.

"Rrrrr female, give me my pleasure." He growled deeply. His hips rose off the bed as he bobbed her head faster. "Yess.." He roared as his juice spurted down her throat.

Robin swallowed as fast as she could not wanting to choke on his cum. She grew more alarmed when he pushed her head forcing her to take all his cock down her throat. She felt it pulsate in her mouth from his orgasm. The noises he was making almost didn't sound human anymore.

Niro pulled her head from his cock then he threw her from him. Robin quickly got up to her knees then froze

Justus Roux

hearing him growl like an animal. He was on all fours and crawling over to her. The look in his eyes was beyond lust as he closed in on her.

"Niro what the hell is wrong with you." Robin jerked back when he roared at her.

"Submit to me." Niro yelled. "Now….rrr female!"

"I don't understand." Robin tried to crawl away from him. He grabbed her and flipped her over pushing her head down on the furs.

"Submit to me." Niro's voice deepened.

"Niro please I don't understand." Robin started to shake. What the hell was going on? She felt Niro's nose in her pussy.

"Your pussy smells so good." His greedy tongue lapped feverishly over her pussy. "Mmm, tastes good." He stuck two of his fingers deep inside her. "Submit to me."

"I don't know how Niro."

"Offer yourself to me."

"Niro please I don't know what you want." Robin felt his hand slap her ass hard.

"Who's pussy is this?"

"Yours." Robin timidly said hoping that is what he wanted to hear.

"Who's?" Niro slapped her ass hard.

"Niro, it is yours Niro." Robin arched her back raising her ass higher in the air.

"Mmm.." Niro buried his tongue back into her pussy. He lapped at every inch then slapped her ass hard. "Do you want my cock?"

Robin spread her legs a little further apart, lowered her upper body onto the furs and lifted her ass as high as she could. "I want your cock, Niro."

"Show me how much." Niro slapped her ass again.

Robin reached under her and rubbed her pussy. She felt Niro's hot breath on her wet pussy lips. "So wet." Niro ran his tongue over her fingers as she played with her clit.

"Please Niro, I need your cock."

Niro stood up and looked at her ass and pussy raised up for him. His eyes followed the movement of her fingers as she spread her pussy lips. "Please Niro."

He watched her shake as he howled. He grabbed his cock and slowly eased it into her. He growled loudly and watched her jerk. He bent over her and pulled her head up. He bit down on her shoulder as he thrust wildly into her.

"Niro." She purred.

"I want to hear your howl female." He rode her fast bit down harder on her shoulder.

Robin felt her body explode, her orgasm so strong she indeed did howl like some wild animal. She screamed out Niro's name as his howls over took hers.

Niro rolled off her and slowly went over to the other side of the tent. He watched the blood trickle down her shoulder. "Don't come near me for a little while." Niro took deep breaths trying to calm himself.

"What is wrong, Niro?" Robin started coming over to him.

"Stay away from me!" He saw the shock look on her face. She didn't understand and he never thought to warn her. Malka men can't be teased to long or their lust consumes them. Robin gasped watching Niro stroke his own cock. He tilted his head back as the cum shot from his cock.

"Niro..." Robin watched his cock grow hard again. She froze when he lunged at her pinning her under him. His cock entered her hard his thrust fast and urgent.

"Niro, you are crushing me." Robin took shallow breaths due to his weight on her. Her hands went to his chest as he arched up and roared out yet another orgasm.

He rolled off her facing away from her. "Niro, tell me what just happened." Robin didn't know what to do.

"I am sorry little one." He quietly said.

"Niro, tell me what happened."

Niro rolled over and reached up for her. He was relieved when she snuggled down on him. "When a Malka male gets to full of lust, he loses control and often times will hurt his mate."

'How does a female…umm help him out."

"By letting him fuck her anyway he needs until he has cum enough to calm himself."

"Okay simple enough."

"Doesn't the males from your planet have such problem?"

"No they don't."

"Did I hurt you, really bad?"

"No, I will be alright. I am just a little shaken up. I will remember not to tease you too much." Robin looked up at him and smiled. "Well unless I want you to fuck me like an animal."

Niro smiled and was relieved and surprised by her acceptance of this. He hugged her tightly as she snuggled against his chest.

Chapter 12

Robin held on to Niro's arm tight as they soared higher in the sky toward the large mountain range. Niro had insisted she wear one of the fur wraps and now she was glad he did. It was much cooler the higher they went up the mountain. Between two mountains laid the Rundal village. The village itself carved into the mountain side the space between appeared to be for crops and livestock.

"Little one, are you going to be okay around so many Rundal?" Niro could sense her uneasiness.

"I will be okay." Robin mentally prepared herself as Ducan landed on a large mountain cliff. Robin took a deep breath as five large Rundal males approached them.

"Greetings Niro." The guard's voice was gentle and soothing a complete opposite to his monstrous form.

"Greetings. I have come to speak with Tomar."

"He is expecting you. Follow me."

Robin latched onto Niro's arm as they followed the large reptilian man. She could feel all their eyes on her, curiosity she imagined. The guard led them into a large labyrinth inside the mountain itself.

"Cave dwellers." Niro whispered to Robin as they entered the dimly lit passage ways.

"Sasha would like to speak with your female later on if this is alright?"

"Of course, whenever she would like."

Robin's eyes opened wide as the narrow passage way gave way to an enormous opened area. "How did they do this?" Robin said in amazement. An entire town was inside this mountain. Rundal of all shapes and sizes moved about. Robin smiled watching the young Rundal run through the walkways. Their young were kind of cute.

"Look a female barbarian." Robin overheard a female Rundal exclaim as they passed.

"Most Rundal have not seen a female of our kind before." Niro quickly explain.

"Now I know what an animal in a zoo must feel like." Robin said.

"Zoo?"

"I will explain later, Niro."

They were led to an elevator. Robin saw more of those strange crystals everywhere. "These give you lights and energy?" Robin asked pointing at the crystals.

"The barbarians were kind enough to show us these. Although a primitive source of energy it is very effective." The guard offered up.

The elevator took them to the top of the village and to a large palace. "Leader hut." Niro said.

"A nice leader hut at that." Robin replied. She still had a firm hold on Niro's arm as they entered the palace. Everything was carved from stones and looked amazing. The different color stone and gems used to make the palace were quite eye pleasing.

"Greetings Niro." Tomar greeted them. Robin couldn't help but noticed none of the male Rundal spoke to her.

"It is against Barbarian traditions for a male to speak with another's female." Sasha's familiar voice filled Robin's mind.

Protector of My Heart

"You can read my mind!"

"I can read your body language. You seemed put off a little." Sasha went to Niro and gave him a big hug. It was certainly a strange sight, especially when Sasha's tail flicked back and forth.

"I believe my mate likes you Niro." Tomar chuckled.

"I am thinking she does too." Robin added.

"Do not worry little female. Mating between Rundal and barbarians will not produce offspring." Tomar gestured to a few chairs off to the side that had fur coverings on them. Obviously just for the barbarians seeing how none of the other furniture had any covering at all.

Robin sat down next to Niro. "Hey wait will not produce offspring. How would you know? So mating between the two races is possible?"

"Most certainly so." Tomar motioned to one of the females. She brought over some water for the barbarians. "However male Rundal have plenty of females so mating with a female barbarian wasn't attempted. But the male barbarian has mated with a Rundal female. Purely experimental."

Robin didn't even want to mentally picture that one. "Who volunteered for that? If I may ask of course."

"Niro and Sasha did upon my request."

"What?!" Robin looked up at Niro.

"Although Sasha was most pleased with the experience, Niro was not."

Niro looked down into Robin's face. "It was favor for Tomar."

"What was it like?" Robin wanted to slap herself for her curiosity.

"I will explain later."

"The Barbarians will become extinct if more females are not found. More males than females are born to them, so this doesn't help them. I offered my mate in the hopes that maybe are two races could mingle. But as I said offspring will not be produce from their union."

"Is it really that bad Niro?" Robin asked.

"I am afraid so, little one."

"That is why I need to examine you Robin." Tomar said. "Will you allow me to test you?"

"Of course."

"Thank you. You are the hope for the Barbarians. Your planet has an abundance of females. I have noticed you look well, so your kind can adapt to the environment on Malka."

"It is like living in the tropics on my planet. You seemed to care a great deal for the Barbarians."

"The Dascon clan has been most generous to us. We have thrived on this planet and as such my race will not die out. I intend to make sure the Barbarians do not die out as well."

"Very noble and generous of you." Robin smiled at Tomar.

ଔଔଔ

"I feel Niro's anxiousness." Sasha said as she and Robin walked through the village. "Does it not bother you?"

"What?"

"Niro being so overprotective."

"Well sometimes."

Sasha started to chuckle. "I think a Barbarian male's concern for his female is touching."

"Don't your males do the same thing?"

"Tomar would protect me with his life, but he doesn't growl at other males just for looking at me."

"It seems you like that." Robin noticed Sasha's tail twitching.

"I do rather enjoy the barbarian male's growl, I have to admit."

"I thought you believed barbarian's to be unattractive?"

"At first, I mean they don't have tails." Sasha turned to Robin and pointed at a stone bench. Both of them sat down. "The things a Rundal male can do with his tail." Sasha sighed. "Anyways, after I got use to the barbarians' strange appearance, I started appreciating them. This happen at the first Trial I went to. This is where I saw Niro defeat all the other barbarians, his first Trial win. As you have no doubt witness Rundal males are not aggressive."

"I have never seen one fight and I was quite surprise none of them enter the Trial."

"A Barbarian would tear a Rundal apart. My people are very peaceful."

"This is a good thing I would think."

"Most of the time. However there is another clan of barbarians who have tried to destroy us. Niro and his father Hakan have sworn to protect us. Hakan has even started to train some of our males to be warriors."

"Not to sound like a catty bitch or anything, but it sounds as though you are in love with Niro."

"No it is not love I feel for Niro. Tomar has all my love. I admire Niro and...." Sasha remembered who she was talking too.

"And what?"

"It would be awkward to talk with Niro's mate about such things."

"Oh... Niro is a wonderful lover."

"That he is. Rundal males are very gentle in their lovemaking, so I was surprised by the way Niro took me." Sasha stood up. "Now let me show you the learning house."

"Okay." Robin didn't really want to hear no more about Niro fucking another female, even if the female was reptilian.

༺༺༺

Robin laid perfectly still on the metal table as Tomar examined her. Being completely naked and having a large lizard man examining her most intimate areas was most unnerving.

"Your birth canal is rather small for a Barbarian offspring." Tomar probe his long fingers deeper inside her. "Your womb is sufficient." Tomar pulled his fingers out and wiped them off. "Tell me does Niro have trouble mating with you?"

"What do you mean by that?" Robin stood up and put her covering back on.

"It is just that a Barbarian male is quite well endowed and your birth canal is a rather small opening."

"It took getting use to but we managed." Robin was getting embarrassed.

"Well I see no real reason why you can't have Niro's offspring. Well of course if you decide to join with Niro."

"I feel kind of funny asking this but..." Robin sat back down on the table.

"Go on."

Protector of My Heart

"Why is it I am not getting pregnant?"

"Ahh, this is easy to explain. The Barbarian male only becomes potent after he joins with a female. During the ceremony he drinks a wine made from a special root simply called the joining root. This triggers something in his body chemistry which causes him to produce ….active sperm for the lack of a better phrase."

"Why that is the strangest thing I have ever heard."

"Maybe strange to you but normal to Niro."

"I guess so."

"Now, why don't you explore our village, maybe journey to the other villages. My home is your home."

"Thank you. I think I will do just that." Robin looked over Tomar as he cleaned up. The phrase not judging a book by its cover sure did fit here. Tomar for what she has seen was a fair, kind and intelligent ruler. More than could be said for some of the rulers on earth.

"Is there something else you want to know."

"Do the Rundal have a joining thing to?"

"Females pick the males they wish to be mates with. If the male accepts her they are mates. No ceremony is needed. I was most honored when Sasha chose me. My love for her can't be measured."

"You seem very happy."

"Blissful."

"Thank you for indulging my curiosity."

"My pleasure."

Robin smiled at him then left the room. Niro was waiting for her.

"I must talk with Tomar, you stay in this village."

"I will try."

"No you will do." Niro had begun to adore that look on her face when she started to get angry. "Please stay in the village." He watched her face soften.

"Okay since you put it that way."

Niro looked both ways down the hallway to check and see if anyone was coming. When he was reasonably sure no one was he grabbed Robin and lifted her up. "My cock hungers for you." He whispered against her lips.

"Niro, we can't do that right here."

"Yes we can if we are quick." Niro pulled her covering up to her hips and quickly pulled his cock from his covering. Robin wrapped her legs around him and pulled him closer to her. His cock filled her, his thrusts were fast, hard and deep; his hands kneading her ass as he rode her.

"Niro." Robin purred wrapping her arms around his neck. Her eyes couldn't leave his face as he arched back and moaned loudly as he orgasm. She pulled his head down closer to her so she could kiss him. "Niro." She whispered as he pulled his cock out of her and gently placed her back down to the ground. She wrapped her arms around his waist and snuggled her face up to his chest. She felt him kiss the top of her head and his strong arms wrapping around her.

"Now stay in this village, little one."

"I will so relax." She kissed him playfully on the nose then headed down the corridor toward the village.

Chapter 13

Rasmus stood just beyond the Rundal village. He watched the trof grazing in the snowy fields. "Demos." He said behind grated teeth. Demos was allowing his conja to get some exercise. "If you are here that means Niro must be as well."

Rasmus pulled back his long golden hair as he continued to watch Demos. He should go kill the troublesome Dascon warrior but he wasn't sure he could overtake him. He signaled back to his men to stay very still. Not only did they have to watch out for Demos but also the Rundal guards.

He waited for Demos to go back inside before he positioned his men. If Niro's mate stepped one foot out into this pasture she would be captured. He might have to wait a long while but Rasmus was a patient man.

CSCSCS

Robin grew accustomed to the stares of the Rundal people. She too, was getting use to their reptilian form. She smiled at the passing Rundal and they nodded their heads in response. She went toward the market place and marveled at the fine pieces of art that were for sale. Her eyes were drawn to the one depicting a Barbarian in battle. His sword was raised above his head ready to strike. Another showed a Barbarian on a conja readying for an attack. Robin looked at the artist, a rather large Rundal male.

"These are very good." Robin said holding the one of the singular Barbarian.

"You like that one?" His voice was as gentle as the other male Rundal.

"This is exquisite." Robin gently placed it back down.

"Then I will make you one of Niro and have it sent to you."

"Oh that is too generous of you, but I thank you anyways."

"Nonsense, it will be a joining present."

Not wanting to insult him Robin graciously accepted his gift. She journeyed further down the path looking at all the wares that were for sale. A strange grunting sound came from the pens further ahead curious Robin went toward the sound.

"Oh, what is that?" Robin exclaimed looking at what could only be described as a very large hairy pig.

"That is a Trof." A Rundal child said. "This is the first time you have seen one?"

"Yes it is."

"They taste really good but are a bit slimy." The Rundal child laughed at the funny face Robin made then went back to his mother.

Robin saw that beyond the pens was light pouring in from the tunnel ahead. "Some fresh air would be nice."

Protector of My Heart

Thinking Niro couldn't possibly mind if she just stood at the entrance for a moment Robin headed toward the light.

ೞೞೞ

Rasmus immediately perked up seeing a small dark-haired woman standing by the entrance to the Trof's pen. He signaled to the two men off to the side. "Come out little female just a little further." He whispered. He looked for Niro and smiled when he didn't see him emerge.

Robin heard a whistling noise followed by the sound of flesh being pierced. She came out a little further to see what had just happen. Her mouth opened wide watching the Rundal guard fall from his watch tower and hitting the ground. Robin hurried over to see if there was anyway she could help him. She fell to her knees in front of the large Rundal guard. He was still breathing.

"Hold on I will go get some help." She saw the arrow sticking out of his back. She decided to leave it in him if she pulled it out he might bleed to death.

"Go back inside the village." His voice was weak, his eyes fighting to stay open.

"I will signal to the other guard, hang on." Robin stood up and started to head toward the other tower.

"Come on mate of Niro, Malin will be most anxious to meet you."

Robin spun around to see a very large golden-haired warrior standing before her. Before she had time to do anything Rasmus latched a hold of her and threw her over his shoulder.

"You think of screaming and I will have to kill him."

Robin arched her back to see Rasmus pointing his sword at the fallen Rundal guard. "I will not scream."

Justus Roux

"Good." Rasmus raced toward his conja. He signaled to his men to join him. He placed Robin in front of him in the saddle then took to the air.

The Rundal guard used the last of his strength to write Niro and Larmat on the ground with his dagger. This was the only thing he could do before he died of his wound.

ઉઉઉ

Niro was beaming from Tomar's news. He and Robin could have offspring now all he had to do was prove to her that he was the best warrior. "We will head back home in the morning." Niro told his men then went out to find Robin. He headed straight for the market place knowing for sure this area would surely peak Robin's curiosity.

Niro greeted all that greeted him as his eyes scanned the area for Robin. He stopped a couple of Rundal children. "Ten ruby for anyone who can tell me where my mate is."

"Don't worry Niro I will find her." The boy said.

"Not if I find her first." The girl added.

Niro smiled watching them scamper off. "Niro." One of the vendors called out to him.

"Mich, I see your talent has not left you yet." Niro picked up the statue of a Barbarian.

"Your mate seemed to really like that one. So I will give her one of you. Do you mind standing still for a moment?"

Niro stood up straight and allowed Mich to sketch him quickly. "I thank you for your generous gift for my mate."

"Your welcome."

"Have you seen my mate lately?"

Protector of My Heart

"She headed over to the Trof pens a couple of hours ago."

"Thank you." Niro nodded and then headed toward the trof pens.

"Niro, Niro." The little boy Rundal hurried over to him.

"Did you find her?"

"Not yet, but someone said they saw her heading out of the trof entrance."

"Stay here." Niro was preparing his lecture for Robin, after all he told her to stay in the village. A trof may look harmless but when provoked can turned into a quite dangerous animal. When Niro exited the tunnel the suns were low in the sky. He looked around quickly and didn't see her anywhere. Relief at first guessing she went back into the village, but panic filled him when he spotted the Rundal guard laying on the ground with a Larmat arrow sticking out of his back.

Niro raced over to him. He checked for any signs of life then he spotted the writing. "Niro, Larmat" he said running his hand over the writing. "Robin!!" He cried out. He hurried back into the village.

"Niro I can't find your mate anywhere." Demos said. He didn't like that look of panic on Niro's face.

"The Larmat were here, they have killed one of the Rundal." Niro's heart pounded. His Robin was taken by the Larmat he was sure that was what the Rundal guard was trying to say. "You two bring the dead Rundal inside so he may be buried properly. Demos go get Tomar and tell him what has happen."

"Where are you going?" Demos grabbed Niro's arm.

"To get my mate back from Malin."

"Nightfall is but moments away the conja will attack you if you attempt to fly."

"I will not leave her with them." Rage and terror filled him; he had to get her back. The Larmat were known for taking Dascon females and doing all sorts of vile things to them. His Robin will not suffer this. "Let me go." Niro growled at Demos.

"If you leave now you will die then who will get your mate back."

"AHHH!!!" Niro's voice boomed through the village.

"When daybreaks we will fly to the Larmat village and get your mate back."

Niro knew Demos was right if he dared to fly now the conja would attack him and Ducan. Demos escorted him back to the palace and made sure he went to his chamber.

"Little one." Niro sat on his bed and try not to think about what was going to happen to her when she got to the Larmat village.

Chapter 14

Robin stood silently next to Rasmus as they waited by Malin's chamber door. Larmat was very similar to Dascon in the way the village was laid out. Robin could feel Rasmus' eyes exploring her body but she pretended not to notice.

"You are small for a female." Rasmus' petted her letting his fingers linger at the ends of her hair. "Tell me are the males from your clan just as small?" He started to twist her hair up in his hand. "Did Niro have much trouble taking you from your male?" He pulled her head back violently then pressed her body next to his. "I will so enjoy hearing your screams."

"Rasmus let the female go." Malin said. Rasmus reluctantly complied.

"You are the female Niro wants as a mate."

Robin wrapped her arms around herself and lowered her eyes to the ground. She could feel the intensity of Malin's gaze.

"You have nothing to fear from me, yet anyways." Malin grabbed her from Rasmus and dragged her into his chamber. "Rasmus tell all warriors that none may touch this female unless I say so."

"Yes." Rasmus growled. He wanted to play with the little female, hell he wanted to break her.

"Leave us." Malin reached back for his sword feeling Rasmus' irritation. Rasmus grunted then left.

Malin released Robin and watched her head over to the other end of the chamber. "Don't fear female, Niro will come for you." Malin poured himself a drink still keeping his eyes on Robin. "Sit down." He smiled watching Robin quickly obey him.

"Why?" Was the only thing Robin could think of to say to the large man. Malin was beautiful with his long golden hair, strong body and handsome face. But Robin could feel his malice. There was no beauty inside this man. Not like Niro who had a warmth to him.

"Why does a female always want to know why?" Malin chuckled. He walked over to Robin amused as she coward back in her seat. He placed his hands on the armrest of the chair and glared down at her. "Look at me." Robin slowly raised her eyes to him. "Why?" He leaned in closer. "Because I fucking hate Niro, that's why you stupid female." He pounded on the chair breaking one of the arms off.

Malin walked a bit away from her. "He will come for you; any Dascon male would do this for his female. That is what makes them weak."

"That makes them noble." Robin quietly replied.

"Noble, hah." Malin rushed back to her pinning her against the back of the chair. "If my female got captured by the Dascon, I wouldn't risk a single warrior to get her back. I am the ruler and can always get another female." Malin grabbed her breast firmly and pressed her harder into the chair. "You are breeders and mere pleasant distractions. Can a female fight? Can a female rule? Can a female even help in the mines or the fields? No, you are but mere pretty objects whose only use is to bring a male pleasure and offspring. So when you are lost you are easily replaced. Fuck the fact your numbers are few the stronger warrior gets the use of females or he simply fucks the weaker, pathetic males who are just about as useless as you."

"Get off me." Robin pushed at Malin's chest. His laughter made her blood boil.

"Do you honesty believe you can challenge me. I would snap you in two." Malin strolled back over to where he sat his drink down. "I will show you what Larmat females are used for." He took a big gulp of his drink. "And when Niro shows up I will tie him up, he will be beaten and bloody but not dead, oh no, he will watch me fuck you over and over…" Malin walked back over to her. "Then I will kill you with my own two hands right in front of him. After he sees you die I will cut him to pieces and send the pieces back to Hakan."

"You are crazy." Robin screamed out.

"Now you are getting the idea aren't you?" His laughter chilled Robin to the bone.

ଓଓଓ

Niro couldn't sleep at all. Robin was with those filthy animals. He knew exactly what Malin was doing and yet he had no choice but to fall into his trap. Robin was his life, his light, his only reason to exist. He could free her; his life was of little consequence.

Unable to take waiting anymore Niro snuck out toward where the conja were stabled. "Shh, Ducan." Niro comforted his pet as he saddled him up. "I know what I ask of you is a lot my old friend, but we have to go now." Niro risked much flying before the suns rose. The wild conja hunted at night. He and Ducan would only have to risk it for a couple of hours. Niro loaded up his bow, though mostly skilled in the sword Niro could use a bow.

"The conja will attack you, Niro." Tomar's voice startled him.

"I have no choice I must go to her."

"Then shall I wake your men?"

"No, I will risk only myself." Niro climbed onto Ducan's back.

"There is nothing I can say that will change your mind? You know it is a Larmat trap. Malin doesn't want your mate he wants you."

"I know." Niro kicked Ducan on the sides and headed out of the stable.

Tomar watched as they took to the air. "Return safely warrior." Tomar said with sadness in his heart. Niro was most certainly going to his death. "Damn." Tomar muttered. What a waste of a good ruler. With Niro dead any warrior could challenge Hakan to be the leader of the Dascon clan, and with the Dascon in turmoil Malin could march in and destroy everything.

ଔଔଔ

Robin winced as the ropes tightened. Malin secured her to a large wooden pole just in front of his bed. "I suggest you don't struggle or the pain will worsen." Malin unfastened his covering and laid out on his bed. He stroked his large cock watching Robin.

"You are vile." Robin hissed.

"Then you should think me evil when I get done showing you what a female is good for." Malin hit a large bell that was beside his bed and in a matter of moments two dark haired women entered the room. Robin noticed the

Protector of My Heart

vacant looked to their faces as they knelt down by Malin's bed.

"Watch mate of Niro." Malin barked. He placed his hands to his sides as the two women crawled onto the bed. "Bathe my cock." Malin hissed. Both women started lapping at his cock. "One on each side of me, I want my guest to get a good view of your tongues on my cock." The women obeyed.

Robin watched them thoroughly bathe his cock with long wet strokes of their tongues, both flicking their tongues over the head of his cock. "You will do this very thing to me." Malin smiled at her pushing one of the women's head down to his balls.

"I would never do that to you." Robin struggled with her restraints. "You fucking bastard."

Malin laughed as he forced his cock into the woman's mouth. "I think we will play a game now, little female." He grabbed the hair of the woman who was licking at his balls.

"I won't play any game with you." Robin hissed.

"Oh I think you will." He pushed down on the woman's head that was sucking on his cock. "Her life will depend on it."

"Alright." Robin quickly said.

Malin released the woman's head and pushed her from him. "Just testing for your weakness female." Malin smiled at her as he bent one of the women over. He entered her with such force she lurched forward. He rode her hard and fast and came quickly he stay in that position as the other female licked at his ass.

Robin closed her eyes and turned away. Those poor women, Robin cringed at the degrading comments Malin shouted at the two women. "Look Niro's female or I can make it a whole lot worse for both of them." Robin watched as Malin shoved his cock down one of their throats and made the other continue to caress his ass with her tongue. The anger, the pity she felt for the two women who were being so brutally used by this bastard. Every nasty comment, every vile act he forced upon them only fed these emotions in Robin. What was worst she was powerless to help them.

It seemed like an eternity before Malin stopped brutalizing the two women. After he came in their hair and all over their bodies he dismissed them.

"I am thoroughly satisfied." He said coming closer to Robin. His hands went to her breasts. "That is what a female is good for, just a mere plaything to amuse a male."

"I hope one of your playthings cut your throat someday."

"Please, no female alive can best me in battle."

"Perhaps not, but one sure could out smart you."

"Ravings of a captive this is all this is. But I admit I do find this most amusing." Malin slid his fingers into her pussy then pulled his fingers out and stuck them in his mouth. Malin went back over to his bed and hit the bell again. One blonde-hair and one dark-haired woman entered. "This is Shea." Malin petted the blonde. "She is my mate and will bear me much offspring." Malin pushed the dark-haired woman to the bed. "This is just Dascon trash."

"Why would a Dascon female be here?" Robin asked.

"She was captured." Malin walked back over to Robin. "Now witness the entertainment these two will bring me." Malin clapped his hands together and Shea laid out on the bed and spread her legs open. The dark-haired woman placed her head between Shea's legs and started licking at her pussy.

"You use the Dascon women as toys." Robin hissed at him.

"That is their purpose." Malin stroked his cock watching the two women.

Robin couldn't watch the Dascon woman being used and turned her head away. She heard Malin grunt and growl then she felt a warm sticky liquid squirt all over her stomach. "You bastard." Robin moved in her restraints.

"You will be covered in my juice before Niro gets here." Malin laughed.

Justus Roux

Chapter 15

Niro pulled his bow back and took aim at the conja that was headed right for Ducan. "Steady boy." He squeezed his legs tighter holding himself firmly in the saddle. He let loose the arrow within seconds the conja's shrill cry filled the air. Niro quickly loaded up another arrow and scanned the skies for more conjas.

Niro commanded Ducan to dive down to avoid the two conjas that were rapidly approaching them. Niro leaned his body down gripping tightly to the saddle with one hand while holding his bow with the other. "Up now Ducan." Niro gripped Ducan tightly with his legs then leaned all the way back shooting the arrow straight up catching the first conja on the underside. Niro tugged to the right so Ducan could dodge the falling body of the wounded conja. Niro directed Ducan to land the beast was tiring and the other conja was quickly catching up.

"Stay hidden." Niro commanded Ducan allowing the beast to catch its breath. He drew his sword and readied for the wild conja. The ground vibrated as the large beast landed. Niro's eyes locked with the beast as he gripped his sword waiting for the right moment to attack. As the conja lurched forward Niro dodged its first blow. He leapt onto the beast's back and embedded his sword in its head.

Niro pulled his sword from the dying beast. He jumped off it and hurried over to Ducan. "Rest for awhile." Niro petted Ducan's forehead. "You have done well." Niro smiled feeling Ducan nuzzle into his touch. Niro sat down on the ground next to him and leaned back into the beast's side. He still had a long ways to go but now with the sun rising at least the conja will not cause too much more of a problem. He tried not to think about what Robin was going through. He couldn't the rage would blind him.

ଔଔଔ

Robin's arms grew weary from being stretched for so long. Her body was sticky and cold. She felt so violated though Malin never took her yet; he just covered her in his seed, which to Robin was worse in a way.

"You are doing well."

Robin looked up and over to the other woman who was tied up similar to the way she was. "How long have you been there?"

"A few hours, Malin wanted more of an audience for his perversion."

"What is your name?"

"Sasa. " The woman shifted her weight. "You are truly the mate of Niro?"

"He is my protector." Robin saw the solemn look fall across the woman's face. "What?"

"Niro has the makings of a great leader."

"This is a bad thing?"

"Now he will die. It will be a great loss for the Dascon clan."

"Why do you say that?" Robin moved her hands in her restraints.

"He will come for you. No Dascon male would leave his female to the Larmat. And when he comes they will kill him."

"Not if he is bringing the whole freaking Dascon army with him."

"He will not. His blinding need to bring you back to safety will cause him to come himself."

"No, Niro is a smarter warrior than that." Robin refused to believe Niro would attempt a rescue on his own.

"Your safety is all that he is concerned about. He is a grand warrior and has no doubt figured out what Malin is after. He knows Malin doesn't want you, he wants Niro."

"No, damn it. Niro won't come alone that is suicide." Robin struggled harder with her restraints.

"My mate Linx stormed through the Larmat village. He brought no other warriors." Sasa began to cry her words begun to shake. "He killed many Larmat warriors before they took him down. Malin sent my beloved's head back to Hakan. But not before he showed it to me."

"I am so sorry."

"Now the same fate will await Niro."

"Not if I can help it." Robin fought violently with her restraints. Her wrist started to bleed as she pulled at the cuffs that held her prisoner.

"You are but a female, what can you do to help Niro?"

"I can help him by getting my ass out of here so he doesn't have to come here in the first place." Robin kept pulling. She used every ounce of her strength. She ignored the pain in her wrist. There was no way she would allow Niro to die. "Which way would Niro come?"

"Niro would choose the path Malin would expect him to come."

"Why?"

"Malin would position his warriors at the other three points."

"Because he believes Niro would try to sneak in."

"Exactly. The southern part of town would be where Niro will come."

"You sound like you have planned many attacks yourself." Robin popped one of her arms free. Then quickly reached up and unhooked the other. When she freed herself she hurried over to Sasa.

"Linx, valued me for the way my mind worked." Sasa replied watching Robin unhook her restraints.

"Then he indeed was a grand warrior." Robin saw the pride in Sasa's face. "Now let's get the hell out of here." Robin scanned the room for any weapons they could use. Malin's swords were just too heavy for them to use but she did find two daggers that would work.

"Come on." Sasa took Robin by the arm and led her to where Malin's women were held. "We have to get some clothing."

"Good idea." Robin quickly followed her being as quiet as possible.

When they reached the bathing chamber Robin had to jump into the bathing pool. She had to rinse off the foul stench of Malin from her body. "Be quick." Sasa whispered.

Robin swiftly got dressed; she wrung her hair out and then followed Sasa. Quietly they went down the corridors. Robin tightened her grip on the dagger. Fear and an urgent need to get to Niro before he reached the village pushed her forward.

Sasa pushed her against the wall just before they left the palace. "Don't move." She whispered.

Protector of My Heart

Robin could hear her heart pounding, the sound of her own breathing was almost deafening as she heard the guard come closer.

"Where are you going?" A deep male voice called out.

"I thought I saw something." The other replied.

"We are not to leave our post. Besides that space is too small for Niro to fit in."

"I suppose you are right."

Robin let her breath out as she heard the guard walk away. "Slowly." Sasa whispered. Robin shook her head and followed her. They had to stop every few feet to make sure the guard wasn't looking toward them.

After what seemed like an eternity they made it out of the palace. "Keep out of sight as much as possible. Our dark hair will cause us to stick out." Sasa said. They weaved in and out of the shadows. Robin observing that all the Larmat was various shades of blonde.

"It is quiet."

"Is that good?" Robin asked.

"Yes, this means Niro isn't here yet." Sasa looked at the two guards who were patrolling the south gate. "We must climb and kill them." Sasa pointed toward the guards.

"I can't kill anyone. There has to be another way."

Sasa looked around the whole area. "If we don't kill them they will alert others that we are escaping."

"Damn it there has to be another way."

"There is no other way, let's go." Sasa gripped her dagger and began to climb the stairway that led toward the guard tower. Robin went to the other side and climbed up toward the other guard tower.

ೞೞೞ

Niro landed Ducan just outside of the Larmat village. "Stay here." Niro petted him then headed toward the village. He knew Malin, and the way he thought. There would be fewer guards at the southern exit. "I love the damn predictability." Niro said seeing only the two guards in the towers. Still he had to be cautious this could be a trap.

Niro pulled his sword when he saw the first guard fall from the tower. A large dark-haired woman had begun to climb down the side of the wall. Niro saw the other guard falling from the other tower; this one flapped his arm as if he was pushed from the tower. He observed the large woman motion to someone in the tower. "Robin." Niro whispered watching the smaller woman climb down the wall.

His heart stopped when he saw two large warriors rushing toward the two women. With speed he didn't know he had, Niro charged at the two males.

"Niro." Robin said. She was surprised when Sasa knocked her to the ground. Before she could speak and asked why the hell she did that. She heard the clashing of metal on metal. When she looked up she saw Niro engaged in battle with two of the warriors.

"Stay." Sasa pushed Robin over to the wall. Niro couldn't be distracted. Sasa kept looking back inside the village; the sound of battle had to be heard.

"Get her out of here." Niro called out. "Head to the wooded area, my conja is there."

Sasa nodded her head and dragged Robin up to her. "I will not leave you here alone." Robin cried out to Niro.

"I will be with you shortly, little one." Niro slashed the throat of one of the guards. He quickly glanced back and saw Sasa dragging Robin toward the wooded area.

Niro concentrated completely on a quick defeat of this warrior. Just as his blade ran through the middle of the warrior a large shadow flew past him.

Niro quickly looked up and saw four conja with riders heading straight toward Robin. Niro raced over toward the women. But the men had already dismounted their conjas and were after the women.

"You never cease to surprise me Niro." Malin said as he grabbed a hold of Robin.

"Let her go." Niro growled.

"You will not bark orders at me Dascon scum." Malin motioned to his men to close in on Niro. "I wanted this to be a long drawn out thing, but it seems your female is cleverer than I give her credit for." Malin grabbed Robin's breasts and squeezed as his tongue snaked up her face. "Don't worry Niro after I have killed you I will fuck the hell out of your female."

Niro howled then charged at the three warriors. Malin backed up still holding Robin to him. Niro swung his sword with such strength he decapitated one of the warriors and then embedded his sword in another's stomach. He quickly grabbed the dagger that was strapped to his thigh and waited for the other to make a move.

Robin tried to break free of Malin's grasp but he was just too strong. She watched Niro dodged the swings of the other warrior's sword. She cringed when Niro's arm got sliced causing him to lose use of that arm.

"Niro." Robin held her breath, praying he would win. She didn't noticed Malin's sword going up to her throat until she felt the cold steel against her neck. He was afraid now; he knew Niro was going to win.

Niro threw his dagger embedding it into the neck of the last warrior. He went over and pulled his sword from the other fallen warrior's gut. "Let my female go." Niro's growl was low and very intimidating.

"Back away or I will cut this bitch's throat." Malin pressed his sword closer to Robin's throat. Niro backed up a bit hoping Malin would relax a little.

Robin swallowed when she felt Malin's sword ease up on her throat. "You are not getting your female back and shortly more of my warriors will descend upon you. Tell me how many can you fight off with just one uninjured arm."

"Let her go and fight me yourself you coward."

"Time to die, female." Malin grabbed Robin by the hair and lowered her to her knees. He pulled her hair and readied to swing. Niro couldn't move there was nothing he could do but watch Malin kill his female.

"You warm my heart, Robin." Niro lowered his sword.

"I love you, Niro." Robin closed her eyes and waited for the blade to strike.

"Touching." Malin laughed. Suddenly he let go of Robin's hair when he felt someone jump on his back, and cold steel against his throat.

"This is for Linx, you bastard." Sasa gasped feeling Malin's sword go through her side but still she dragged her blade over his throat. Blood spurted outward as he fell backwards onto Sasa. "A female...took...your life. Your father....laughs... in paradise." Sasa said in his ear as both of their lives slipped away.

"Little one." Niro hurried to her and scooped her up into his arms. Robin felt him wince.

"Put me down you are hurt."

Niro gently placed her down and checked her for injuries. "We better get out of here, little one." Niro grabbed her hand, but she stopped him when she looked down at Malin and Sasa. Robin reached back and closed Sasa's eyes.

"Robin." Niro gently pulled her forward.

"Let's go home." Robin's heart burst seeing his smile. Something she thought she was never going to see again.

"Get him, now." Rasmus yelled.

Niro latched onto Robin's hand and dragged her to the wooded area where Ducan was waiting. "Get on, little one." Niro saw the arrows embedding into the trees around them. The Larmat warriors will shoot them from the sky.

"Robin." He gently caressed her face then he strapped her to the saddle.

"What is that look for?" Robin looked deeply into his eyes. "Oh no you don't…" Robin struggled with the restraints. "No Niro! Come with me now."

"Demos will make a good mate. He will protect you well."

"I want you Niro, please come with me." Tears filled her eyes. "No damn it we made it, please Niro, please…"

"They want me, little one. Once I show myself they will not notice Ducan flying away." Niro kissed her deeply, letting her feel all the love that was in his soul for her. "I love you, Robin." He slapped Ducan and ordered the beast to take Robin back to the village.

"Niro!!!" Robin yelled as Ducan took to the air. She watched as he charged out of the wooded area. All the warriors instantly focused on him. "Niro…" Robin fell forward and wrapped her arms around Ducan's neck.

Chapter 16

Niro fell to the ground to exhausted to continue. Robin was safe; Ducan would get her back to Dascon by nightfall.

"I want to kill the son of Hakan." He heard the warriors starting to fight amongst themselves to see who could lay claim to the deathblow.

Niro forced himself up to his feet. He will meet death standing proud. He focused on the two warriors who were fighting. He tried to lift his sword but was unable his muscles couldn't give anymore.

"I get the honor of killing you, Niro." The biggest one in the group said proudly. Rasmus had left this group of twenty warriors to finish off Niro. With Malin dead Rasmus wanted to secure his place as leader.

"Then try to kill me." Niro growled standing tall with his last bit of strength he raised his sword in a fighting stance.

"Shame really you have fought will son of Hakan." The large warrior closed in on Niro. Thoughts of Robin filled Niro's mind. The tender way she kissed, touched and made love to him. *I love you Niro*, her sweet voice echoing through his head as he waited for the warrior's blade to slice him.

Justus Roux

Whistling sounds raced through the air. Niro watched several arrows embed themselves into the oncoming warrior. Niro looked up and saw Demos with two other Dascon warriors swooping down, riding on the back of conjas. Demos' conja flew down and he scooped up Niro throwing him behind him on the saddle.

"I told you not to come without us." Demos scolded him. "Where is your female?"

"Safe." Niro leaned into Demos. "She is safe."

"You are the next leader of Dascon. Don't ever do something so fool hearty again."

"Robin is my female I had no choice but to rescue her." Niro started to laugh.

"What is so funny?"

"She would of escape all on her own. Isn't that amazing?"

"She probably knew stupid you would charge in there alone. Your mate is brave for a female." Demos reached back and secure Niro to the saddle. Niro looked badly injured.

"No Demos, she is brave like a warrior."

"You rest now. I don't know if we will make it back to Dascon before nightfall but we will try."

"Your conja is the fastest in all of Dascon. We will make it."

෴෴෴

Robin jumped off Ducan the second he landed. She rushed through the leader hut right for Hakan's chambers.

"Where is Niro?" Kelila said rushing toward Robin.

Protector of My Heart

"You have to gather some warriors Niro is still at Larmat fighting a whole mob of warriors." Robin watched as Kelila turned white and sunk down to the floor.

"What is wrong?" Hakan quickly went to his mate's side.

"Niro." She clung onto him. "Is dead."

"No he isn't damn it." Robin went to Hakan. "Please order some warriors to go help him."

"It will be nightfall soon." Hakan held his mate tight.

"Don't leave him alone with them." Robin pulled at Hakan's arm.

"He is dead." Hakan shook Robin.

"No he isn't, damn it, I would feel it if he was."

"It is touching the hope you have Robin, but Niro is more than likely dead by now." Hakan pushed her away and returned his arm to his mate.

"Then I will go help him!!" Robin screamed at both of them and rushed out of the leader hut back to the stables.

"Your conja is tired." The stable hand said as Robin tried to saddle up Ducan.

"Then find me another one. I have to help him." Robin followed the eyes of the stable hand as he looked up toward the sky. Four conjas landed.

"Demos!!" Robin yelled running out to him. He would help her she knew he would. "Niro is in trouble."

"Calm yourself female." Demos climbed off his conja and untied Niro. He had passed out miles ago.

"Niro!" Robin yelled seeing Demos throwing him over his shoulder.

"He will not hear you. Go tell Kelila to prepare the healing room."

Robin ran her hand through Niro's hair. He looked beaten and bloody but he was alive. She ran as fast as her legs could carry her back toward Kelila.

"Niro is alive!" Robin yelled down the corridor.

"I have told you this can not be so." Hakan grumbled.

'Demos has him. He said to get the healing room ready."

Kelila immediately came to her feet and headed down the corridor. Robin hurried after her. "I want to help." She said as they entered the room.

"Start lighting the candles." Kelila handed Robin a strange stone. Robin saw the candles that were positioned all around the large bed. She walked over to one and waved the stone around. A strange glow filled the stone and in a matter of seconds the candle lit. Robin was amazed that the stone didn't burn her hand; it just felt warm against her hand. She quickly went around and lit the rest of the candles. A spicy scent filled the room. The fragrance instantly calmed Robin down.

Kelila filled a bowl of water with several different herbs. She mixed all the herbs and water up and then waited patiently for Niro. "Go ready a messenger for Talmor." Kelila told the large warrior who entered the room. He nodded his head then quickly left.

Robin backed away from the door when Hakan and Demos carried Niro into the room. He still hadn't regain consciousness. This worried Robin. A fear engulfed her like she never felt before. Niro couldn't die, he just couldn't. The thought of living on this strange world without his warmth terrified her. She looked up at Demos as he stood guard by the door. She couldn't love him the way she loved Niro. A sick feeling wrenched at her stomach, she couldn't even picture living without Niro. Thoughts of Charlie filled her mind. She thought she loved him, hell she was even happy at their wedding, comfortable with the life they had together. But never did her love for him fill her like this, made her fear consume her just by the mere thought of being without him. She grabbed Niro's hand. This strange wonderful Barbarian lover was everything she wanted, hell he was her soul.

Kelila sang a beautiful melody as she washed Niro's wounds with the water and herbs. A song a mother would sing to her sick child. Robin choked back the tears watching Kelila tend to her son.

"We will have to wait for Tomar." Kelila ran her hands through Niro's hair. "Niro is strong…" Kelila ran from the room not wanting others to see her tears.

Demos stepped outside to give Robin a moment alone with Niro. "Hey you why don't you wake up and let me see those beautiful green eyes of yours." Robin gently stroked his cheek. She looked down his body the wounds were many; he had to of lost a lot of blood. She squeezed his hand but his hand remained limp in hers. "Please Niro wake up." Robin nuzzled her face against his cheek.

"Tomar will come." Demos said as he relit one of the candles. "You must eat."

"I am not leaving him." Robin sat up but still had a hold of Niro's hand.

"You will need your strength to heal him."

"I am not leaving." Robin's eyes didn't leave Niro's face. Demos saw the love in Robin's gaze. It made his heart heavy wishing he had a female who loved him as much. He quietly left the room knowing she wasn't going anywhere.

Robin moved Niro's hair out of his face. "Did you hear that barbarian? Your female isn't going to eat anything until you wake up. And I know you wouldn't want me to grow weak from hunger. After all you are my protector aren't you?" Robin climbed into the bed with him and carefully snuggled against him. "Please Niro wake up. I love you."

Chapter 17

Robin felt a warm hand on her shoulder, when her eyes fluttered opened her gaze met with an older man's. "Who are you?" She sat up.

"This is Sage." Kelila said. "He will tend to Niro until Tomar arrives."

Robin quickly got out of bed and let Sage do what he came for. Robin saw three warriors standing by the wall. The first one came up and sat down next to Niro. Sage took a long tube with a large needle in it and attached it to the warrior's arm; he then placed the other end of the tube into Niro's arm.

"Sharing of one's spirit." Sage said anticipating Robin's questions.

Robin watched as the warrior's blood began to flow into Niro. A new hope filled her. Working at the hospital she had seen her fair share of blood transfusions but not quite like this. This would give Niro hope. She watched as warrior after warrior came into the room offering up part of his spirit to help Niro. Sage stopped after five warriors making sure not to take too much from any one of them.

"This is all I can do, Kelila." Sage stood up. Though his hair was a silvery gray color and his face had a few wrinkles his body was just as strong looking as the younger warriors. "Keep talking to him." He said to Robin before he left.

"His coloring is better." Kelila said kissing Niro gently on the cheek. "I will return when Talmor arrives."

"If you would like to spend some time alone with him, I can wait outside." Robin said.

"He needs you more than he needs me." Kelila smiled at Robin then quietly left the room. Robin went back to sitting next to Niro. She gently grabbed his hand and offered up a silent prayer.

ඎඏඏඎ

"Robin." Sabrina's familiar voice pulled Robin from her daydream.

"Sabrina." Robin welcomed her hug.

"Has he spoken?" Saa asked. He stood off to the side looking at Niro laying there.

"No, he hasn't woke up yet."

"He will, soon I bet." Sabrina said in a cheery voice. "We brought something that might bring him around." Sabrina motioned to Saa. He let in three older women.

"The singers." Robin exclaimed. She grabbed Niro's hand as the women started to sing. It was the same Rundal song Robin heard at the banquet.

"It's the first song I ever heard here, so I figured it was for you too." Sabrina said wrapping her arms around Saa. "So I hoped that it might wake Niro up."

"It was a wonderful idea." Robin smiled at her. She listened to the haunting melody remembering Niro translated the song for her. She gave Niro's hand a squeeze. She felt him squeeze back.

Protector of My Heart

"Niro." She brought his hand to her lips and kissed it gently. "I guess this would be our song in a strange way, huh." She felt him squeeze her hand tighter. Tears welded up in her eyes. He could hear her. "I love you Niro."

"Little one." The sound of his voice was more beautiful to her than the goddess like voices of the singers.

"Niro." She cupped his face in her hand as his eyes opened up. "Your eyes are so beautiful." She barely got the words out. Relief rushed through her body.

"We should go tell Kelila and Hakan." Sabrina said.

"I knew you wouldn't fall easy." Saa said as he smiled down at Niro.

"Saa." Niro was still very weak and was tiring out.

"Come on let's get his mother before he falls asleep." Sabrina dragged Saa out of the room.

The singers stopped singing. "Please continue." Robin asked. The older woman nodded her head then they started singing again.

"You scared me." Robin kissed him lightly on the lips. "Don't ever do that again." She started kissing all over his face.

"I am so tired." Niro said trying hard to keep his eyes open. He was so happy Robin was uninjured.

"Niro." Kelila sat on the side of his bed. She grabbed his hand and kissed it then held it to her face. "You must rest. Don't tire yourself to much."

Niro nodded then closed his eyes no longer able to stay awake.

Robin wiped away the tears from her eyes. She grabbed a sheet and covered him.

"You should rest." Kelila said.

"I will."

Justus Roux

Kelila kissed Niro's hand once more then sat it down. She got up and left the room.

"Thank you." Robin said to the singers when the song ended. She waited for them to leave then she crawled into bed with Niro. She snuggled up next to him. She almost cried again feeling his arm wrap around her pulling her closer to him.

ɷɷɷ

Robin paced around the room stretching her legs. "Tomar." Robin bowed her head with respect as he entered the room.

"Robin." Tomar nodded his head back. Three other Rundal males came into the room carrying a strange silver cloth. Robin went to the back of the room to give them some space. She watched as they covered Niro with the strange shimmering cloth. Tomar injected Niro with two needles full of an orange colored substance. After Tomar was finished he stepped back and allowed the other Rundal males to wrap Niro up like a mummy in the silvery cloth. Tomar cut a slit where Niro's mouth was.

"Tomar?" Kelila said entering the room.

"Niro has some bad internal bleeding. Leave him in the healing wrap for two days."

"Will he be alright?" Kelila asked. Robin moved closer eager to hear the answer herself.

"I believe so."

"Thank you." Kelila said.

"Yes, thank you very much." Robin added.

"It is the least I could have done for my friend." Tomar bowed his head then left the room followed by the other males.

Protector of My Heart

"You must rest Robin." Kelila said. The devotion Robin showed to Niro was touching to Kelila.

"I will rest in here." Robin sat down on a chair next to the bed.

"I thought that is what you would say." Kelila motioned to the warrior standing in the hall. He brought in a couple of furs and pillows and positioned them on the floor just in front of the bed. When he was done he left.

"I will see you in the morning." Kelila smiled at Robin before leaving the room.

Robin looked at the silver mummy that was Niro. She placed her hand on his chest. She could feel the heat of the fabric. A medicine smell wafted up when she removed her hand. "Good night Niro."

Justus Roux

Chapter 18

Robin was awoken by the sound of tearing fabric. Her eyes adjusted to the brightness of the room. "Niro!" She exclaimed watching him break out of his silver cocoon.

"AHHH!!" Niro cried out when he burst free of the cloth.

"Niro?" Robin slowly walked over to him. There were no longer any cut marks on his body. He wasn't pale or tired looking anymore. He looked as he did before he was injured.

"Little one." He opened his arms and Robin fell in them.

"You are okay." Robin burst into tears, mostly from relief.

"Please don't cry…" Niro became very upset.

"I am just so happy you are okay." She wrapped her arms around him tightly. "But how…and so fast." Robin ran her hands up and down his body amazed that there were no marks or anything. She touched a piece of the silvery fabric, it was smooth and slick feeling.

"The Rundal are very skilled in the art of healing." Niro stated.

"I would say so." Robin made a mental note to thank Tomar and to ask him about the wrappings.

Justus Roux

"I need to bathe." Niro smiled down at Robin. "I will need your assistance."

Robin jumped out of bed and straight for the bathing chamber. She readied his bath before he came in. She smiled watching his cock harden as he entered the bath. Oh yes, he was feeling better. Gently she bathed him paying extra attention to his large cock. Her body was reacting to the feel of his hard cock in her hands. She should really let him rest, she gasped when his arms gripped her waist.

"Little one." Niro lifted her up and settled her down on his cock. Slowly he entered her. He leaned back enjoying the warmth of her pussy as it sheathed his cock. "Stay like that." He said when all of his cock was buried in her wetness. He kept his cock buried deeply in her pussy as he stroked her back. His eyes locked with hers the heat of their gaze caused him to start thrusting. He watched the pleasure that swept across her face as she moved her hips up and down.

"Niro." Robin sighed as he gripped her hips and helped her ride his cock. He raised his hips up matching her stride. He watched as her hands went to her breasts kneading and stroking. "Niro." She purred as her fingers flicked across her nipples.

Niro growled as his orgasm hit him quickly. "I am sorry." He quietly said. He knew she didn't have her pleasure yet.

"It is alright." Robin leaned into him and laid her head on his chest. The warmth of the water and the sound of his heart beating soothed her. "I am so happy you are alright. This was just a bonus." She smiled sweetly up at him then laid her head back on his chest.

Protector of My Heart

ෲෲෲ

"Niro!!" Kelila exclaimed as she wrapped her son up in her arms. She stepped back and looked over his body. "You must eat something and build your strength." Kelila motioned to the two smaller men and they hurried off. "Where is Robin?"

"Right here." Robin came into the dining hall with a platter of food. She sat it down next to Niro.

"She takes good care of you." Kelila patted Niro's hand.

"Yes, she does." Niro smiled at the loving way Robin set up his dinner for him. Though he was quite capable of doing this himself he felt she somehow enjoyed doing this for him.

"Eat all of that. Kelila is right you have to build your strength up." Robin sat down next to Niro as he devoured the food.

Niro was famished and ended up eating everything that was brought before him.

"Wow you can eat." Robin exclaimed watching him polish off the last of the fruit platter.

"Dascon males have very healthy appetites." Kelila added. "Robin I wish for you to come with me there is something we need to discuss. Niro you need your rest anyways."

"I have rested enough. I need to train."

"Oh no you don't." Robin stood up and cleared the plates away from the table she handed them over to the very petite man. "You came very close to dying. No, no you will go rest."

"I will go train." Niro stood up and stretched out.

"No, you will go rest." Robin stood there with her arms crossed giving him a stern look.

Niro smiled he loved the look on her face when she was angry. "Little one, I need to train. "

"You will go rest, damn it."

"Robin, why don't you come with me now, Niro knows the limits of his body." Kelila gently guided Robin toward the door. She knew Robin wasn't going to win this argument with Niro. He was very serious when it came to his training.

"Promise me you won't push it, okay." Robin said.

"I promise, little one." Niro went to her and gently kissed her lips. He liked this kissing it seemed so intimate and gave their sport a much deeper meaning.

"Niro, she must come with me." Kelila gently pushed him back from Robin.

"Little one." Niro stroked her face then reached over and kissed his mother on the cheek.

"Remember you promised not to train to hard." Robin said watching him grab his sword.

"I will not train to hard. Now go with my mother and do female things."

"What? Female things, now what the hell does that mean." Robin couldn't help but smile hearing Niro's laughter as he left the room.

Kelila led her down the hallway and to a very elaborately decorated chamber. "Wow!" Robin exclaimed. Finely detailed golden walls gave the room a very soft look to it. There was a large bed with soft white furs covering it. All the furniture had different furs covering them. Robin ran her hand over the large sculpture of Hakan; the soft stone from which it was formed from gave the piece life. Other small pieces of sculptures were all over the room, conjas, Rundals and warriors in various states of battle were the subject for the artwork. Another large sculpture of Kelila stood by the balcony of the room as if to beckon the visitor to go out onto the balcony. Robin did, the view was spectacular, and the two golden towers seemed to frame the distant mountain range.

"This is my private chamber. Hakan made this for me years ago." Kelila joined Robin out on the balcony.

"He did this for you?"

"Yes, he wanted me to be surrounded by beauty and to have a space that was all mine."

"That is so…"

"I have never thought of the right words to thank my mate for this wondrous gift. No words I could think of seemed enough to show him what this meant to me."

Kelila gently guided Robin back into the room. "Now we have an important matter to discuss, Robin." Both women sat down in two large chairs.

"Okay."

"First off, let me say I will not be angry or upset with you." Kelila motioned to the warrior in the doorway. "Could you bring us some tea?" The large male nodded his head and went out of the room.

"How did you know he was there?"

"Hakan always posts a guard by me." Kelila reached up and took the tray from the warrior. "Thank you." He nodded his head then went back to his post. Kelila handed Robin one of the cups. "Have you given thought to who you will join with?" Kelila sipped her tea. She silently hoped Robin had decided on Niro.

"Is this joining like marriage? I am unclear just what joining means."

"I know not what your word marriage means, but I can tell you what joining means. When you agree to join with a warrior; you agree to be his mate. He must protect and cherish you. He must also provide for your well being and that of any offspring you will bear him. Your happiness is his responsibility. "

"Hey wait, what does the female do in the relationship?"

"His happiness is your responsibility. You provide him with offspring and care for them. "

"What if a female wants to work outside of the hut?"

"What?"

Robin stood up and paced around. "Say what if I wanted to work in one of the healing rooms or maybe be a teacher. Is this allowed?"

"Oh, I see what you mean. The Clan is most important. Everyone who lives within the Dascon clan must care for one another. Everyone tends to the sick or teach the young etc."

"What of the weaker males?" Robin cringed by thinking of those poor men treated like sex toys.

"Robin, everyone has a purpose in the Clan. Those men were given a chance to prove if they could serve the clan in any other way. Have you not noticed the helpers that roam through the hut?"

Robin thought about this. She did remember seeing some of the smaller men around the grounds. "Do they have to watch out… you know…"

"From being raped by stronger warriors?"
"Yes."

Protector of My Heart

"They are not bothered when they serve in huts or on the training grounds. Only the ones in the weaker male's hut are used as females."

"But they don't get females either, do they?"

"Unless they challenge a protector and win."

"Well I don't see that happening."

"Getting back to the main subject." Kelila smiled, she loved Robin's curiosity. "When you join with a male, you are joined forever."

"Then it is like marriage." Robin sat back down.

"The sooner you are joined the safer you will be. You remember what I had told you earlier about no male being allowed to touch another male's mate?"

"Yes, I remember."

"Have you decided on a mate?" Kelila held her breath waiting for Robin's response.

Robin didn't have to think long. "I want Niro to be my mate." Robin was surprised when Kelila grabbed a hold of her and hugged her hard.

"We have much to discuss." Kelila sat back down, she couldn't be happier. Robin would make Niro very happy. "The joining ritual is a long process. This is to ensure that the female is certain of her choice."

"Okay what's involved?"

"All males have two weeks in which they will challenge Niro for you. This is their last chance to do so."

"Well I don't think anyone will challenge Niro."

"Oh, don't say that. The more males that challenge Niro for you the more honor you bring him."

"That is the stupidest thing I ever heard."

Kelila started laughing. "It is a male thing. I thought this tradition was pretty stupid myself."

"How many warriors challenge Hakan for you? That is if you don't mind my asking."

"Let's see. I believe twenty warriors challenged him during those two weeks."

"Holy shit! You must have been the bell of the ball."

"I don't understand."

"Never mind, it would take to long to explain. So what happens if no warriors challenge him?"

"This hasn't happen. So I wouldn't know."

"Okay so I won't lose sleep over that one. Anything else happens in the two weeks?"

"You will prove that you can satisfy Niro's male needs."

"His male needs. Oh I get it I have to fuck his brains out for two weeks." Robin smiled thinking that wouldn't be difficult to do.

"Well it is more than that. You must be creative." Kelila stopped for a moment trying to think of how to put this. "Give him a sample of the pleasures you will bring him."

"Okay be kinky. I got it. Anything else?"

"The night before you are officially joined you will perform the dance of seduction at a feast."

"What?!" Robin's mouth fell open. No, she must have heard Kelila wrong. There is no way Kelila just said that she would have to strip at a freaking dinner. "Could you repeat that?"

"You will perform the dance of seduction."

"Just what in the hell is that?"

"You will start; you must seduce every male in the room just by your dance. After you have done this and Niro feels the sexual tension grow he will join you in the dance."

Protector of My Heart

Robin didn't know what to say. Her body despite her best efforts otherwise got aroused just thinking of Niro doing a dance of seduction. "What does Niro do during this dance?"

"He is suppose to seduce you until you take him right there in front of everyone."

Robin's pussy grew wetter thinking of Niro's glorious body dancing just for her.

"Doesn't sound all that bad does it?"

"No, it doesn't." Robin couldn't get the sexy image of Niro out of her mind.

"Then the next morning, you and Niro will be officially declared each other mates."

"Is the ceremony long?"

"No, Niro just will say the sacred words then place his bracelet on your wrist."

"What do I do?"

"You offer your wrist to him; this signals that you accept him as your mate and life time protector."

"Poor Niro seems to be the only one risking so much, you know."

"That is the lot of a Dascon male. They must prove worthy of a female's warmth."

"How do I tell Niro that I want to join with him?"

Kelila smiled. "Offer yourself to him and say I want you as my mate."

"He will know what I mean right?"

"Oh yes, but it never hurts to be creative." Kelila poured Robin another cup of tea. She could see the curious look in Robin's eyes. She would want to know more details about everything.

Chapter 19

Robin lay in Niro's big bed waiting for him to return. She had positioned herself several times trying to look her sexiest. She was naked with the fur barely covering her breasts. She decided to lay on her side with her legs positioned so her pussy was covered.

She held her breath when she heard the door open. Slowly she looked up. Niro was letting his eyes feast on her body. He undid his covering letting it fall to the floor his eyes never leaving her.

"Niro." Robin purred stretching her body out, letting him see her pussy. She heard his growl as he approached the bed. "Wait." She held her hand up stopping him from touching her. She stuck her finger in her mouth and let her tongue snake around it, all the while looking Niro in the eyes. She got her finger good and wet then brought it to her clit. Niro's eyes lowered down watching her finger tease her sweet clit. Another growl escaped his lips as his cock grew harder and more demanding.

"Niro." She whispered getting up on all fours and crawling to the other side of the bed.

Niro growled again and climbed on the bed. "Wait." Robin locked eyes with him. "Stand up on your knees." Niro instantly did what she asked. His breathing became more rapid as his body screamed at him to take her. Robin crawled over to him and grabbed his cock firmly in her hand. "Mmmm." She said licking her lips. She ran her tongue over the head of his cock. She felt Niro's hand go to her head. "No, keep your hands by your side." He did, at this moment he would do anything she asked of him. Robin ran her tongue down the entire length of his cock then back up again. "Niro." She sighed. She took the head of his cock into her mouth and gently sucked letting her tongue flick back and forth at the same time.

"Robin." Niro moaned clenching his fist. He felt her take more and more of his cock into her mouth. He could feel her tongue lapping at the same time she sucked on him. The sensation was mind-blowing; he had to grit his teeth to stop himself from cumming.

"Niro." She purred, her saying his name so seductively was driving him mad. Robin placed his cock between her breasts. She squeezed her breasts together creating a soft tunnel for his cock. Niro began to thrust he couldn't stop himself. Robin licked at the head of his cock as it emerged from the tunnel she created with her breasts.

"Don't stop." Niro's voice begged as he felt her pull away from him.

"Niro." Robin cooed. He opened his eyes and saw her laying back into the bed. Slowly she opened her legs. With two fingers she spread her pussy lips apart. "Niro, I want you to be my mate."

"Robin…" Niro went to her; he gently entered her all the while looking deeply into her eyes. "I will be honored to be your mate." His words broke as he spoke. He dreamt of this moment, now that it has happened it didn't seem real. He felt Robin wrapping her arms around his neck pulling him down to her.

Protector of My Heart

"Make love to me." She said against his lips. He kissed her soulfully as he slowly thrust his cock deeper into her. He propped himself up on his elbows placing as much of his body weight on her that she could stand. He needed his body as close to her as he could get. The softness of her and the heat of her kiss were heavenly to him. She wanted him as a mate this thought warmed and filled his heart. She was his, all his forever. His emotions bubbled up inside him, the sheer joy of this perfect moment. He felt the wetness of Robin's tears against his cheek. He opened his eyes and look down at her. Her tears rolled down her face as her body arched up in response to her orgasm. "Niro I love you." She screamed out as she rode the waves of her orgasm.

"Robin." He lay down on her wrapping her in his arms. "You warm my heart; you are my heart, little one." He whispered in her ear. He thrust faster until his own release engulfed him. It took everything he had to contain the emotions that swirled inside him. He lowered himself down so his head rested against her heart. Robin wrapped her legs around him and her hands played through his hair. He didn't want to move. He wanted to stay wrapped in her warmth eternally.

෴෴෴

"Congratulations!!" Sabrina exclaimed hugging Robin tightly.

"I hear that congratulations are in order for you too." Robin smiled at her friend then looked up at Saa who was puffed up with pride.

"Yep, me and this big lug are tying the knot, or slapping on the bracelet in Malka terms." Sabrina smiled up at Saa. "Can I talk with Robin alone? Besides you and Niro have to…whatever you males do to congratulate each other."

"Don't leave my sight." Saa said.

"Oh I won't." Sabrina waited until he went over to Niro. "Did Kelila tell you what was involved with this joining thing?"

"Yes, she did."

"Rather kinky don't you think? Not that I am complaining. It beats the hell out of a bridal shower and the formal rehearsal dinners back on earth."

"Are you nervous about the dance of seduction thing?" Robin asked.

"A little, but at the same time it sounds kind of hot."

"When are you and Saa going to be officially joined?"

"Around the same time you and Niro are. I wonder if we get to dress up. These coverings are nice and all but I have never been married before a wedding dress would be nice."

"I have been married before but I can see your point. I am sure we are supposed to wear something special." Robin jerked around when she heard Niro growl and pull out his sword.

"What the hell?" Sabrina said as Saa grabbed her and pulled her over to him.

"Jerris challenges Niro for Robin."

"What?" Robin recognized the large warrior; he was the one who guarded Kelila the other day. "Please tell me they won't kill each other?"

"They battle until one proclaims the other the better warrior."

"Well geez why don't they just whip out their cocks and we can measure them." Sabrina rolled her eyes.

"Like hell you will." Saa rumbled.

"Relax baby it is just a figure of speech." Sabrina reached out and grabbed Robin's hand giving her a little comfort as she watched Niro and Jerris fight.

Within moments Niro had his sword at Jerris' throat. "You are the better warrior I concede." Jerris said.

Niro sheathed his sword and helped Jerris to his feet. "Good fight." Niro said. Both men nodded their heads in a show of respect to one another then Jerris left.

"You guys are so polite with one another." Sabrina wrapped her arms around Saa's arm. "This warrior has fought two other big dudes so far protecting my honor." Sabrina said in a southern accent.

Robin chuckled then smiled watching Saa standing there proudly. Sabrina had a wonderful sense of humor which went well to balance out Saa's seriousness. Robin watch Saa tense up then she quickly followed his eyes to see what he was looking at.

"I challenge you Niro for your female." Demos' voice boomed through the room. Robin watched Saa relax which caused her to become very nervous. Saa was obviously afraid Demos was here to challenge him. Which means…Demos was someone to be feared.

Niro pulled his sword. He had just fought Jerris would he still have the stamina to take on Demos. He ready himself as Demos charged at him.

Robin felt Sabrina grab her hand again as they watched the battle. Both men were equally as skilled. Robin squeezed Sabrina's hand hard.

Niro blocked Demos' attacks and volley a few of his own. He waited for the right moment to push the attack. With Demos there might not be a momentary weakness or mistake. Niro felt his arm vibrate as Demos' sword clashed with his. Demos spun around and struck again this time missing Niro completely. Niro lunged at Demos the moment he waited for was here. With a sweep of his leg he knocked Demos to the ground he quickly climbed on top of him and placed his sword to Demos' neck.

"You are the better warrior, Niro. I concede."

Niro quickly climbed off Demos and helped him to his feet. "Good fight." Niro bowed his head to Demos. He sheathed his sword and went over to Robin.

"A moment." Saa said to Niro stepping to the side of the room.

"What is it?"

"Demos let you win." Saa said. "He never makes a mistake like that."

"I know Saa."

"Why?"

"He wanted to honor my female." Niro and Saa exchanged knowing looks and then went back to their females.

"Let's get out of here. I am tired out." Niro wrapped his arm around Robin's waist and guided her out of the room.

Demos watched Niro and Robin leave the training area. His heart was heavy. He could have won; Niro had just battled before hand. But he had too much respect for Niro and the little earth female to take her from him.

Chapter 20

A week had passed and Robin fucked Niro in every possible way she could think of, so far anyways. Niro had fought off ten other warriors who wanted Robin. Niro at this same time commissioned the building of a hut just for Robin and him. He gave her full reign over the whole project.

"Sure of yourself aren't you my big bad warrior." Robin said as they stood at the site the hut was going to be built on.

"No male will take you from me."

"Mmmm, I love it when you talk like a Barbarian." Robin said playfully. She looked over the beautiful view they had being perched there on a top of the hillside. "You chose this very spot to build the hut, just for me?"

"Yes." He walked behind her and wrapped her in his arms. "Are you pleased?"

Robin leaned back into his embrace. "Yes, it's beautiful up here. But…"

"If something is not right I will change it. You need just to wish for something and I will acquire it for you." Niro nuzzled his chin to the top of her head.

"I want what makes you happy as well, Niro."

"What makes you happy also brings me joy."

"That is not what I mean." Robin gently removed his arms from her. "I want to know what makes you happy Niro, so I can acquire it for you."

Niro smiled down at her. "I am happy just to be around you."

"That is beautiful Niro but what else."

"I don't understand what you want me to say."

Robin sat down on the grass and patted the spot next to her. "Sit down."

"Alright." Niro sat down next to her.

"What if I told you I didn't want you to battle anymore?"

"Then I wouldn't."

"But you would be unhappy. You have trained many years to be as good as you are. I bet you like going out there and protecting the village. I even bet you go help the smaller villages out who is part of the Dascon clan."

"Of course I answer their call for aide. They are my people."

"But yet if I asked you to stay with me all the time and not go to the aide of your people you would do it."

"If you ask it of me I would do it." Niro turned her face gently so she could look him in the eye. "You would not ask anything from me that you knew would make me unhappy."

"How do you know this?"

"I know you, little one." He lowered his lips to hers and kissed her tenderly. Robin wrapped her arms around his neck and pulled him closer.

"But Niro I want you to argue with me if we disagree about something. I don't want you to let me have my way all the time."

Protector of My Heart

"If you wanted to do something that would bring you harm I wouldn't allow it." He kissed her nose playfully. "Then you can argue with me all you want over it. But if I know something will bring a smile to your face I will acquire it for you." Niro stood up and stretched out. "You are welcomed to battle me and if you win then I will concede." Niro was caught off guard when Robin leapt at him and knocked him to the ground.

She grabbed his arms and pinned him to the ground. "Do you concede?"

"To what?" He chuckled.

"To letting me ride that big cock of yours until we both get off."

"Mmm I concede, you may do with my body as you will."

"Stay like that." Robin jumped off him and rushed over to the stakes in the ground. She pulled two out along with the length of rope they had attached to them. She went back over to Niro and raised his arms above his head. She twisted the rope around his wrist then placed the stakes into the ground securing him.

"No hands." She said as she slowly removed her covering. She let it slip from her body inch by inch watching Niro's eyes as he followed the journey of the cloth down her body. He pulled up on the rope pulling the stakes from the ground. "Oh no you don't, if those stakes come up again I stop what I am doing." She leaned over him letting her breasts hang down into his face. She felt him trying to reach up to take the nipple into his mouth. "Remember if the stakes come up you don't get off." She smiled when Niro only nodded his head.

"Taste me." He rumbled.

"Patience." She kissed down his muscular chest taking her time. She knew the more she teased him the wilder he would become an aspect of Malka males she was growing to love. She let her tongue slip inside his belly button making Niro squirm. "Ah a bit ticklish are we?" She said flicking her tongue over it again. She brought her mouth over to the leather strap that held his covering in place. Grabbing it with her teeth she pulled on it until it became untied.

"Taste me, female." Niro thundered.

"I'm getting to that part." She pulled his covering from him throwing it off to the side. "This is a beautiful cock." She ran her tongue up the entire length. "A tasty cock." She licked the precum from the head. "A big fucking cock." She wrapped her hands around the shaft loving the feeling of it, hard yet soft and warm. "You want me to swallow all of it?" She flicked her tongue over the head.

"Rrrrr, do it." He wanted desperately to break free and grab her head as she fed on him. But he didn't want to chance she would stick to her threat to stop if he did break free.

"Yum, yum." She let her tongue roll over the head once more before she took his cock into her mouth. She positioned herself between his legs then slowly inch by inch swallowed his enormous cock. She felt it slide down her throat as his pubic hairs tickled her nose.

"Oh damn....female....mmm." He arched his back as he felt her nurse on his cock but still keeping all of it down her throat. Slowly she came back up the shaft, sucking and licking all the way up. "Please!!!" He cried out needing release. He tried thrusting his hips upwards but she pinned him to the ground. She continued slowly

Protector of My Heart

sucking up and down his shaft making sure to take it all each time. "Please, damn it, ahhh!!!" She brought him right to the edge then stop just before he fell over. She did this over and over. Niro felt his orgasm build again as she continued this exquisite torture. "Make me cum!!!!" He yelled as he hovered on the edge. "Yesss!!!!" He screamed as she allowed him to cum. His juice filled her mouth and she eagerly drank it down.

"Arrhhha, come here." Niro broke the rope that held his wrist. He threw the rope and stakes away then lunged for Robin. He pulled her up until he could reach her pussy with his mouth. Robin could barely keep her balance as Niro held her in an almost standing position. He spread her legs so her feet were firmly on the ground now. Robin held on to his head to keep her balance. His tongue greedily lapped at every inch of her pussy. His hands cupping her ass he rubbed her pussy over his face as his tongue tasted every part of her.

"Niro...oh..." Robin closed her eyes and enjoyed the sensation of him sucking on her clit. Her eyes popped open when he smacked her ass hard.

"Rub your pussy on my face until you cum." Niro said slapping her ass again. Robin grabbed handfuls of his hair and pushed him closer to her. She rocked her hips back and forth rubbing her pussy on his face. His tongue flicked back and forth in time with her hips.

"Niro..yes..yes.ahhh!!" Robin tilted her head back and closed her eyes, she held Niro firmly to her. "Niro..." She felt his tongue dart in and out of her opening lapping up her honey. "Fuck, please, please fuck me." She felt herself being lifted up then forced down to her hands and knees. Niro stood up and lifted her hips up forcing her to stand on her hands. He plunged his cock into her, thrusting hard and fast. Robin gasped when he lifted her up cupping her breasts with one hand and wrapping the other arm around her waist. He was standing up, thrusting his cock deeply into her. She felt his arm tighten around her moving her faster up and down on his cock all the while kneading her breasts with his other hand.

"Cum for your male." He said breathy in her ear. "Cum." His hand went to her clit he stroke her at the same rhythm he thrust.

"Yes, Niro!!!" Robin screamed as she climax.

"Reach behind and wrap your hands around my neck." He said moving both hands to her hips. Robin arched back and held on to his neck. He moved her up and down on his cock faster and faster, grinding his hips into her at the same time.

"Cum now Niro." She said feeling another orgasm building. She heard him grunt and growl as he moved her hips harder and faster until he buried himself to the hilt inside her roaring out his orgasm.

"Little one, mmm" He lowered them slowly to the ground. He cuddled up against her back covering her with his body, warming her, making her feel safe.

"You broke the rope." She playfully scolded him. She loved teasing him so he would lose control and fuck the hell out of her.

"Next time I will try harder not to."

Robin lay contently in the warmth of Niro's embrace as the suns rose in the morning sky.

Chapter 21

"Look at this fabric." Sabrina held a shimmering gold cloth.

"Oh, I love that." Robin exclaimed running her fingers over it. "I want this one for my wedding…umm…joining covering.

"Good choice with your brown hair it's perfect. Now to find something that goes with this." Sabrina pointed to her auburn hair.

"Your hair is beautiful. Let's see…" Robin picked through all the fabric Kelila had brought in. "Something really shiny." Robin picked up cloth after cloth holding it up against Sabrina. "Perfect." She said holding up a piece of silver cloth. "Look how it plays in the light."

"You're right." Sabrina held the fabric up to her in the mirror. "I am going with this one."

Both of them handed their choices over to the older woman. She took the fabric out of the room. "Do you miss earth?" Sabrina asked as she picked up a cup of tea.

"No, surprisingly I don't." Robin sat down across from her. "I feel bad that I don't miss my husband at all."

"Well having a man like Niro keeping you warm at night, I can see why you don't miss your husband." Sabrina saw the solemn look cross over Robin's face. "Did you love your husband?"

"At first, very much so, of course I was very young when we met. Am I a bad person for not missing him...for loving Niro..."

Sabrina sat down on the floor in front of Robin and reached up for her hands. "Listen." She squeezed Robin's hand. "You are not a bad person for wanting something more. If you truly loved your husband you would have been fighting to get back to him."

"That's what I am ...."

"Hey just be quiet and listen. I see how happy you are when you are with Niro. Were you this happy with Charlie?"

Robin thought for a moment. "No, I wasn't."

"Okay let me put this another way. Say Charlie some how managed to come here and he took you from Niro what would you do?"

Robin remained silent for a moment. "I would fight to come back to Niro."

"There is your answer. If Charlie was the one, you know your soul mate you would have fought the whole Dascon army to get back to him. But instead you try adjusting to Niro's world. So I would say Niro is your soul mate." Sabrina stood up and went over to pour herself some more tea. "You can't fight what was meant to be. So, forget about Charlie and enjoy loving Niro."

"Thank you Sabrina." Robin smiled grabbing the cup of tea Sabrina brought over to her. "What about you, do you miss earth?"

"No, I didn't have anyone."

"No one?"

"My boyfriend just dumped me, my parents weren't talking to me and I was way behind in my bills." Sabrina started to chuckle. "So when a very large, hot barbarian dude busted down my bedroom door, I didn't fight him or cared where he was taking me. It sure the hell had to be a better place than where I came from."

"Do you love Saa?"

"I am marrying; oops joining with the big lug ain't I." Sabrina smiled. "Yeah I love him more than I thought I could ever love a man."

"So I would say we both don't miss earth all that much." Robin added. Both women started laughing.

૭૩૭૩૭૩

"Niro." Hakan greeted his son. "Sit down." He motioned to the chair across from him.

"What is so urgent?" Niro sat down.

"I have had word that Rasmus is now the leader of the Larmat clan."

"He is a sick sadistic bastard. How did he stake claim to leadership?"

"He murdered Malin's mate and their offspring." Hakan got up and grabbed the map. He spread it out over the table.

"He killed all of Malin's offspring?" Niro went over to his father.

"Yes."

"But they were so young, some were but babies."

"Niro your compassion pleases me, but also shames me."

"I don't understand."

"I wasn't sadden by the lost of Malin's offspring. You however still have empathy in your soul, something I am lacking in my advance years."

"No you grow to melancholy in your advance years." Niro grumbled. "Now continue telling me of Rasmus."

"He placed the bodies all over Larmat territory daring anyone to challenge him for leadership. A few did and lost; he took their bodies and displayed them for all would be challengers to see. He was named ruler a few days ago."

"He will be a bigger threat than Malin was. He knows no fear."

"Tell me Niro what you would do with the information that you know now."

Niro looked over the map. "I would station look outs all along the borders. I would also station some warriors in a permanent outpost by the Rundal village."

"That is what I have done." Hakan looked over at his son. Niro was ready to assume leadership of the Dascon clan. But Hakan knew his son wouldn't challenge him, Niro would never want to bring shame to his father.

"Then all is well, why did you summon me here?"

"I wanted to see what you would have done." Hakan sat back down. "Plus it is getting closer to your joining day. Are you prepared for it?"

"I just wish it would hurry up and get here, so I can make Robin my mate."

Hakan laughed loudly. "You sound like me before I joined with your mother. Let's drink to your soon to be mate." Both men lifted their glasses in a toast.

Chapter 22

Robin was so nervous, today was the joining feast. She looked at the sheer fabric she was supposed to wear. "I might as well be naked." She was forbidden from seeing Niro these last two days and she missed him terribly.. another sign that she had made the right choice by asking Niro to be her mate; after all there was no such thing as divorce here on Malka. Kelila had explained this all to her as they shopped for all sorts of things for the new hut.

"Once you have chosen a male for a mate there can be no other. If you lay with another male, your mate will kill you both and he would be in his right to do so. Same if he lays with another female, you can have him executed." Kelila's words echoed in Robin's head as she looked at herself in the mirror. The sheer white cloth did little to cover her body.

"They take the death do you part very serious here." Robin said to herself. She sat down on the bed and waited for Kelila to bring her to the chambers where the feast was being held. Sabrina had already left to go to her joining feast. Robin wished she could peek into the chamber where Sabrina was performing just to see what was going on. But the chamber Robin was supposed to go to was clear at the other end of the hut.

Justus Roux

"Are you ready?" Kelila said as she entered the room.

"I am not sure." Robin's nervousness was mounting. She didn't know if she could dance seductively in front of a room full of warriors.

"Your friend was nervous just like you are now, but she is doing very well."

"You looked in on her? Tell me what is she doing?"

"I only peeked in to make sure she was alright and she is doing wonderfully, Saa should be very pleased."

"What am I suppose to do? Will you look in on me?"

"You just let the music take hold of your body and dance as if you are dancing only for Niro. And no, I will not be looking in on you." Kelila chuckled a little. "Niro is my son; this would be odd to look in on his joining feast."

"Oh I see your point."

Kelila grabbed a hold of Robin's hand gently. "When I did this I dance only for Hakan. I imagined we were in his chamber and I was trying to seduce and tease him until he was so worked up in a frenzy that he....well you know how Dascon males get."

"Thank you." Robin hugged Kelila tightly. "You have been so helpful and kind to me since I have arrived. I don't know if I would have figured out the difference between our two planets without you. "

Kelila smiled brightly and fussed with Robin's hair. "Well after tomorrow you will be my daughter. Hmm, the one I always wanted."

The emotion of the moment threatened to make Robin cry. Kelila was so accepting of her, more so than Charlie's parents ever were.

Protector of My Heart

"Now let's get you down to that joining feast, the sooner you start your dance the sooner you will become more relax and maybe even enjoy yourself."

Kelila led Robin out by the arm towards the joining feast.

಄಄಄

Niro sat in the center of the large room. He was dressed only in his covering and nothing more. This was the one time he didn't have his sword or dagger with him. His eyes darted around looking at the other ten males, them too only wearing their coverings. Everyone sat on mounds of fur for their comfort. Directly in front of them was a large open space for Robin to perform her dance. Tables sat off to the side covered with food and drink; in the corner of the room were the female musicians.

Niro snapped to attention when music began to fill the room. The beautiful voices of the musicians seemed to illuminate the room with radiance and splendor. His mouth fell open when Robin entered the room. Her small, curvy body easily seen through the sheer covering she wore. Her hair was brushed to perfection. Her eyes locked with his as her body began moving to the seductive melody. Her hips swayed and rolled as her hand wandered down her body all the while her eyes stayed focused on him. Niro heard the grunts and growls of the other males as they watched her dance. His cock painfully hard watching the sensuous way she moved. He watched her slowly pull up the sheer cloth revealing her glorious body for all the males in the room to enjoy.

Robin stayed focused on Niro. This dance was for him and only him. Her hips rolled, her hands journeyed down her naked body. She became more aroused when she heard the growls of the other males. For the first time she allowed herself to look around the room. All the males in the room were focused on her; this intensified the erotic feeling she had. She watched as some let their hand's slip into their coverings so they could stroke their hard cocks. The look of pleasure and hunger on all their faces excited her.

Niro saw Robin taking enjoyment from the hungry looks of the other males, this was his sign. He stood up and slowly made his way to her. He let the music soak into him. He had to seduce her into fucking him right here in front of all these horny males.

Robin froze as Niro came closer his strong body moved with the music. Her eyes drank in his image. His hips moved in an inviting manner, beckoning her to him, promising her pleasure. She watched as his hands slowly traveled down his body heading for the ties to his covering. Painfully slowly he pulled at the ties, teasing and summoning her to him. She moved forward unable to stop her feet, never had she seen a man move so seductively before; her eyes unable to leave his cock as he grinded and thrust to the music. Her pussy grew wetter with each inch of flesh he revealed. She wanted to reach out and pull the damn covering off him. He reached for her and pulled her to him as his covering hit the ground. He grinded up against her back as she faced the crowd her body moving with his in a frantic pace. The males howled as Robin went to her knees then lowered down on her arms lifting her ass to Niro. He fell to his knees behind her and entered her with one quick thrust.

Robin's eyes shot open when she felt a pair of hands on her breasts that weren't Niro's. She felt Niro pull his cock out of her and soon it was replaced by another male's.

"What?" Robin closed her eyes and let the sensation wash over her as she felt someone's tongue slip into her pussy. Three males were pleasuring her. She opened her eyes to see Niro sitting back stroking his cock as he watched the three pleasure her.

"Niro." She called out. She watched as he leaned his head back and shot his cum all over the platter in front of him. Robin felt another pair of hands on her. She heard the male who was fucking her roar as he pulled his cock from her. He too cum on the platter Niro did. Another male entered her while another gently guided her mouth to his cock. Robin reached out her hands and grabbed any cock that was next to her. She stroked, sucked and fucked at all four males each one pulling free of her the moment they came, and each cumming on the same platter the others have.

After every male had cum the platter was taken to the feasting table. Robin felt herself being laid down and a tongue began lapping at her pussy. She looked down and saw one of the males enthusiastically bathing her pussy with his tongue. He lapped at her until she had a most amazing orgasm. As she laid catching her breath another male began lapping at her pussy. Each one of the ten males brought her to orgasm. Niro came to her and turned her around forcing her head to the ground and her ass up in the air. He rammed his cock into her, thrusting as hard and fast as he could. He leaned over and bit her shoulder keeping her pinned under him.

"Scream, little one, show them I bring you the most pleasure." Niro growled into her ear as his cock slammed into her even harder and faster.

"Niro!" She cried out feeling her orgasm building, each thrust of his cock intensified it until...."NIRO!!!!" She screamed out. Her orgasm so intense Niro had to hold her up or otherwise she would of collapsed on to the ground.

"Ah, ah!" Niro cried out thrusting faster and faster. "Oh yes, my female!!" He roared. He pulled his cock from her and sprayed his cum all over her ass, like an animal marking his territory.

"Little one." He pulled her to him and cradled her in his arms. He kissed the top of her head then got up and walked over to where his covering was. After he put it back on, one of the musicians handed him a black embroidered covering for Robin. Niro carried the garment over to her then went to his knees and held it up to her. Robin looked down at him, his head was bowed as he knelt there before her, and in his outstretched hand was the garment. Robin gracefully took it from him. He rose up and helped her put it on.

One by one each male brought over some sort of food or drink, each falling to his knees before her offering her what they had in their hands. Robin ate and drank what they brought her. The room was silent. Only when she had finished did the music began to play again.

Robin observed the platter that held all the males semen being taken from the room by a smaller male. "Niro, what is he going to do with that?" Robin whispered over to him.

"It goes to feed the flowers you will be carrying tomorrow in the joining ceremony."

"Okay..." Robin thought that was a bit strange and made a note to ask Kelila the significance of it. "Niro did I do well?"

Protector of My Heart

"You have shown me great honor this evening, little one." He brought her hand to his lips and gently kissed it. "You warm my heart." He smiled up at her.

"I love you Niro." Robin snuggled into his embrace as each one of the warriors quietly left.

Justus Roux

Protector of My Heart

Chapter 23

"You know I feel funny asking this but…" Sabrina adjusted the gold circlet on her forehead.

"But…" Robin was finishing having her hair curled up.

"Last night at your joining feast did you…well…get ravished by a pack of horny warriors?"

"Yes." Robin saw the blush on Sabrina's cheek. "Did the warriors come all over a platter?"

"Oh my God yes!" Sabrina hurried over and sat down next to Robin. "What do you supposed they did with the platter."

"It goes to feed the flowers you will be carrying today." Kelila's voice made both women turn to the door.

"What was the whole joining feast about? I thought I was suppose to do a little bump and grind, then Saa got up there and worked it for me until I fucked him in front of all those males. But oh my God what happen after that I sure the hell wasn't expecting."

"Me too." Robin added.

Kelila sat down on the chair across from them. "As I explained once you are joined with your mate there is no touching another male."

"So that was like a one last, get every guy that I might have fucked in my lifetime done all in one night thing." Sabrina said quickly.

Kelila chuckled. "In a way yes, your dance was to inspire lust. When Saa or Niro joined you in the dance they were to inspire your lust; the energy from your bodies calling for one another feeds the room. After you offered your body to your mate and he takes you, he then relinquishes your body to that energy that has been built up in the room. He spills his seed as an offering to the life that you and he will share. The other males offer there seed as a blessing to this new life. That is why their combine seed goes to feed the flowers you will be carrying; for once you toss the flowers in the flames the energy from that night is released, blessing your joining."

"Okay in a strange way that makes sense, but what was with all that kneeling and offering of stuff." Sabrina asked.

"It was the males' way of showing their respect for you that your body was not used then simply discarded. That is why Saa or Niro in your case Robin was the first, they were offering you back your modesty. The other males offer food and drink to restore the energy back to you that you had given to them."

"So it was like they were saying thanks for the good time, honey." Sabrina asked.

"Oh no, it means so much more than that. Yes, they want to thank you for giving them pleasure but it also shows their respect for you. They don't want the female to think any of them thought lesser of her and that they hold her in the highest regard."

"Okay I think I understand." Robin said. Her hands fidgeted nervously in a few short hours she will be joined forever to Niro. She will never see earth again. Some of the Dascon customs were strange to say the least. Oh, she loved Niro she never doubted that but did she really wanted to be treated like a porcelain doll. What real role did women play on this planet, other than breeders and givers of pleasure?

"What is wrong Robin?" Kelila said seeing the confusion in her eyes.

"How does life change for a female after they are joined, other than not being afraid of getting attack by some horny warrior?"

"Robin you think too much." Sabrina stated. "The way I see it, I have a big gorgeous barbarian dude, he loves me and can fuck so good, mmm.... I digress; he is going to take care of me for the rest of my life. He won't cheat on me, so I don't have to worry about him chasing other women behind my back; and if he does I get to kill him. He treats me with respect, kindness and love." Sabrina went over to the window. "Look how beautiful this planet is. There are no freaking power lines strung up everywhere, no billboards, cars, or tons of rude people. Sure some of what these people do is a bit strange, but sure the hell not as bad as some of the shit I have seen on earth. So I think I am the luckiest woman in the world and I am going to finish getting ready and then march down the aisle and become Saa's wife. So if you will excuse me." Sabrina grabbed her brush and headed over to where a couple of smaller males waited to doll her up.

"Your friend put things pretty well I think." Kelila said.

"I see her point, god do I see her point, but I just have to know how things change. Will I be able to make a difference in this world?"

"You already have."

"How?"

"You bring a smile to my son's face. He has never been happier."

"Niro." Robin whispered standing up and going over to the window. This world was beautiful there was no denying that.

"You can teach the young, help our elders." Kelila gently touched Robin's shoulder. "Niro will be leader shortly he will need your wisdom to help him make the right decisions."

"Sasa." Robin quietly said remembering the strong Dascon female who helped her escape from Malin.

"She was a brilliant strategist."

"You knew her?"

"Yes, her mate Linx was one of our greatest warriors. He proudly let Sasa help him with battle strategy; to him they were a team. Just because our males treat us like fragile flowers doesn't mean they see us as less than them. It is in a male's nature to protect his mate."

"Well then I better get ready, I wouldn't want to be late for my own joining ceremony." There were no more doubts left in Robin's mind. She knew she loved Niro and he loved her that was all she needed to know.

"You remember how the ceremony will proceed?"

"Yes, I practice all last night."

"Than I shall go on to the joining chamber, I am sure Niro is feeling a little nervous himself." Kelila lightly kissed Robin's cheek then left.

Robin sat down on the chair and let the smaller males do up her hair as she rehearsed what she was supposed to do in her mind.

Protector of My Heart

Robin felt her stomach doing flip flops as she came closer to the chamber were the joining ceremony was being preformed. Her hands tightened around the bouquet of brilliant red color flowers. When she reached the chamber doors they were slowly opened for her by two of the warriors she had pleasured the night before. They bowed their head to her as they held the doors open for her.

When she entered her breath caught, Niro looked amazing. He had on a black leather version of his loincloth. A silver dagger was strapped to his thigh; the hilt of the dagger was elaborately carved. The strap of his sword's scabbard that lay across his chest also had elaborate carved silver details attached to the leather strap. His sword hilt had been polished. His bracelets seemed to gleam in the sunlight and the silver band he wore on his forehead illuminated his green eyes. He looked like a mythical warrior, a dream, her dream.

Niro couldn't take his eyes off of Robin. She looked beautiful, her golden covering wrapped around her body softly showing off her curves. Her sandals were covered with jewels and shimmered with each step she took. The fire red color of the flowers she was holding made her blue eyes dance. The circlet she wore framed her beautiful face giving it an amazing glow. Niro thought his heart would burst. This female was his, all his, for the rest of his life.

The room fell in silence when Robin reached Niro. Robin bowed respectfully to Niro and he did the same for her. She turned and bowed to the elderly male who was to be witness to their joining. Robin then turned her attention back to Niro. He pulled his sword from its sheath; he gripped the hilt and pointed it to the ground then offered it to Robin. She gently placed the point of the sword on the ground and held the hilt firmly with one hand.

Niro fell to one knee and bowed his head. "I offer you my protection; my sword is a token of that." Niro looked up holding his breath. Robin lifted the sword up and gently kissed the hilt before handing it back to Niro. He slowly let his breath out; she took his offering of protection. He gracefully sheathed his sword remaining on bended knee. He bowed his head again. "I offer you my body to use for your pleasure. I offer you my heart, so you can bask in the warmth that fills it. I offer my life to you to do as you will. My sword that you have accepted will protect you from any danger. My mate, I give to you my soul and everything that is mine." Niro took the bracelet off his left wrist and held it firmly in his hands. "In your eyes I have proven I am the strongest warrior, that I have the ability to protect you and our future offspring. Do I also have your heart, body, and soul?" Niro's heart raced as he waited for her response.

"Niro, I give you my heart, body, and soul and give myself over to your protection." The words shook as Robin spoke them. She gracefully extended her right arm.

Niro rose to his feet and gently placed his bracelet on her wrist giving it a gentle squeeze so it would fit.

The elderly male came over to them carrying a golden goblet. "For all here let it be known that Niro and Robin are now and forever joined. Niro by drinking this sacred juice, your seed will produce offspring. May your young be strong and wise." Niro took the goblet from him and drank down the liquid.

Robin squealed when Niro lifted her up and threw her over his shoulder carrying her out of the joining chamber. She could hear the cheers from all in the room as he carried her to his chamber.

He kicked open the chamber doors then gently placed her back on her feet. He stood by the bed waiting. Robin closed her eyes and tried to remember what Kelila told her to do. She walked over to the fireplace where a large fire was burning, the flames giving off a warm glow through the room. She kissed the flowers then threw them into the fire. As the flowers burn blue sparkles rose up from them. "Wow." Robin whispered looking at the beautiful colors of the flame. She turned around and slowly walked over to Niro who was still standing by the bed.

"My mate." Robin purred.

"Forever, little one." Niro softly said as she began to take off his dagger. She carried it over to the fireplace and sat it down in front of the fire. She did this with his sword and silver head band. She went over to him and slowly untied his covering letting it fall to the ground. She took two steps back from him and begun removing her covering.

"Is it okay to taste you first before we have each other?" Robin asked coyly.

"Grrrrr." Niro reached over and pulled her to him.

"I take that as a yes." Robin smiled up at him as she lowered to her knees. She ran her tongue up and down his cock, letting it roll, flick and lap at him. His hands tangled in her hair as he leaned his head back enjoying the sensation of her tongue.

"Suck me." He barely got out; his cock was so hard it ached. He moaned feeling her mouth take in his cock. The slurping, sucking sounds she made as she enjoyed giving him pleasure drove him right to the edge. He had to count backwards and think of anything other than what she was doing to his cock to keep himself from cumming.

"We have all night Niro. Let me feed on your juice."

"Yes...." Niro tightened his hands on her head feeling it bob faster on his cock. "Suck louder....oh yes..." The sounds of her sucking on him filled the room. She cupped his balls and gently kneaded as she continued to suck on him. Niro breathed harder as his orgasm build. "Don't stop....please...oh yes, YESS!!!" He screamed.

Robin gulped down all the juice that pumped from his cock. This time it tasted different. Instead of the salty tang, his juice was sweet like candy. She nursed his cock for every last drop of the tasty juice. "Yummy." She said standing up licking her lips. "That was the tastiest cum I have ever ate."

"The joining ceremony drink changes my seed." Niro lifted her up then laid her gently on the bed.

"So your cum will taste like candy from now on, not that I mind the way it tasted before or anything."

"Yes." Niro lowered his head between her legs. "Your pussy taste sweet to me." He growled as he buried his face in her pussy. His tongue probing everywhere, he lifted her hips up so his tongue could swirl around her rosebud.

"Niro..." She cooed. His tongue flicked and circled her anus before journeying back up to her pussy. With long wet strokes he bathed her pussy. He flipped her over and raised her hips up to him. He buried his face in her pussy, licking and lapping at her hole, darting his tongue in and out before letting his tongue flick across her clit. He moved his tongue down the length of her pussy then went back up to her anus, letting his tongue swirl around and around causing Robin to get dizzy with pleasure.

"Niro, yeesss…." She moaned. She felt his fingers circling on her clit as his thumb went into her opening, his tongue still circling her anus. "Mmmm, ahh, yes." Her orgasm build and build. "Please don't stop Niro…" He kept his efforts up enjoying her moaning and the way her thighs started to quiver, he knew she was climaxing. He stood up and plunged his cock deep into her. "Niro!!!" She screamed. The feeling of his hard cock thrusting in her right after a spectacular orgasm was nirvana.

"Ride me." Niro growled smacking her ass.

"Fuck me hard, really hard." Robin said slamming her hips back into him.

"Rrrrrrahh, I'll fucking ride you hard." Niro grabbed her hips tightly and rammed his cock in her as hard as he could. The force made her lurch forward. He climbed onto the bed on his knees still thrusting hard into her. He got himself in a squatting position behind her as he continued to ride her. He leaned forward.

"Do it Niro, oh god do it." Robin moaned

Niro pulled her up to him by her hair his teeth latched onto her shoulder. He started growling like a wild animal as he continued to thrust hard into her. His thrusts became faster and more violent as he bit into her shoulder pinning her to the bed.

"Niro I am going to cum, oh yes yes…."

Niro came back up to the squatting position as he roared his climax still thrusting into her. When his cock was drained he fell onto the bed pulling her into his arms. "Did I hurt you?" Niro ran his fingers over the bite mark on her shoulder.

"I asked you to do it." Robin turned around and snuggled up against him. "I just love it when you get all animal on me."

"You are all mine." Niro wrapped his arms around her holding her tightly against him.

"Yep, you are stuck with me forever."

"And I couldn't be happier."

"What happens now?" Robin looked up into his eyes.

"Well my mate, I plan on fucking you all night."

"After that silly."

"We live here until our hut is ready."

"How about when you are the leader?"

"We live where we want to." Niro pulled her up so he could kiss her. His kiss was gentle and sweet. "Our offspring will fill the hut, strong males like me and beautiful females like you."

"How many offspring are you planning on me popping out for you?" Robin playfully nipped at his nose.

"As many as you can manage." Niro nuzzled his face against her's.

"So protector of my heart, how would you like me to take you now." Robin ran her fingers up his sculpted chest.

"Protector of your heart, hmm, I like that." Niro cupped her face in his hand. "You warm my heart, Robin."

"I love you Niro." She kissed him softly.

"There is still so much to see and do in this world and you will have to show me everything."

"Of course."

"But right now…"Robin climbed on top of him and eased his cock into her.

"My body is yours, little one." Niro smiled at her as she slowly rode his cock.
THE END

July 2004
Keeper of My Soul
By: Justus Roux

Miranda Williams lived a normal life until a tall, blonde, handsome stranger named Michael Varzor appeared in her life. He wasn't your ordinary run of the mill stud muffin, but one that could leap four stories into the air, run at mind numbing speeds, and oh yeah, who hunted demons for a living.

Miranda is quickly pulled into Michael's world when he has to protect her from a demon named Syn. Miranda can't believe that this sub world exists. Michael has to be crazy or even more terrifying that his tales of Heaven, Hell and Purgatory are true. Endanger of losing her mind and her heart Miranda must believe in her instincts and trust Michael.

Michael Varzor was a paid killer in his mortal life but after his death, he was pulled from the grayness of Purgatory by a man named Asurul. Michael was trained to become a demon hunter so he can protect Asurul's son Ayden. Suited for a life of a hunter Michael had learned long ago to numb his feelings. He swore to never love another woman again, never to give a woman that kind of power over him. But one look at Miranda sends him into a spiral. Wrestling with his pass and trying to fight the present Michael now has to battle with a demon that is stronger and more cunning than any before. Michael must allow Miranda into his heart or both of them will lose their souls.

Justus Roux

Protector of My Heart

My Master
Written by Justus Roux

The Books that make up the Master Series explores all levels of sexuality. My Master introduces readers to this erotic world, an island paradise where guests are free to explore their sexuality. A man called Master rules, his sexual magnetism so strong no one can resist. His pets, a group of attractive men and women help guests live their sexual fantasies. No one is judge the only rules are everything must be consensual, leave no one wanting, and Master's word is law.

I only want to bring you pleasure- Master Drake

Jessica Scott was timid when it came to sex. The sting of her husband's betrayal was still fresh in her heart. But Master will opened her eyes to all sorts of sexual delights and show her what love is really meant to be.

Master had the ability to put any man or woman in a delicious erotic spell. All couldn't wait to please him. Though Master cared deeply for his male and female pets, it took Jessica to show him what love was.

Both go on an erotic journey of love, lust and everything in between.

Available now
www.justusroux.com for sample chapter

Justus Roux

Printed in the United States
90932LV00001B/82/A